FRANCHISEMENT
THE ALAN GIBB STORY

How To Make It Yours

DONALD DEWEY

MILFORD HOUSE

an imprint of Sunbury Press, Inc.
Mechanicsburg, PA USA

MILFORD
HOUSE

an imprint of Sunbury Press, Inc.
Mechanicsburg, PA USA

For information about special discounts for bulk purchases, please contact Sunbury Press Orders Dept. at (855) 338-8359 or orders@sunburypress.com.

To request one of our authors for speaking engagements or book signings, please contact Sunbury Press Publicity Dept. at publicity@sunburypress.com.

ISBN: 978-1-62006-340-8 (Trade paperback)

Library of Congress Control Number: 2019950735

FIRST MILFORD HOUSE PRESS EDITION: January 2020

Product of the United States of America
0 1 1 2 3 5 8 13 21 34 55

Set in Bookman Old Style
Designed by Crystal Devine
Cover by Lawrence Knorr
Edited by Lawrence Knorr

Continue the Enlightenment!

For all PAST, PRESENT, and FUTURE TAPS members.

CONTENTS

INTRODUCTION

I N THE EVOLUTION of the human species personal relationships have never been so mottled with insecurity and fraught
with peril as they have been at the dawning of the millennium.
Rare is the day the average gendered individual does not feel his
self-lapsing into angst or her spirit being enveloped by ennui
upon exposure to somebody else. Miscommunication, inadequacy,
conflicting tastes in cereals, and entirely different thoughts on the
part of two or more people thrown together—all these phenomena
identify social chasms hourly. Other people remain other people;
they are not Us.

At the same time, the Us remains invisible in our mirrors. What
we see, at best, is a single form requiring technical assistance in
more areas than we care to count. And though we might resist being
defined by what we see, we see nothing else. Yearning for a higher
purpose in our lives founders on everything from the squattings of
negative cynicism to the eviction of positive imagination. When we
tell ourselves to forget about a higher purpose, to be satisfied with
the self-fulfillment due solely to *Numero Uno*, we worry we won't
be able to count that high. Our 12-step programs to physical and
moral recovery have shaky banisters, our 10 Commandments seem

like any other Top Ten list, and we keep forgetting what the score is. Together with the problem that other people remain other people, we suffer from the doubt that we may or may not even remain Us.

What has lent special drama to our plight is the backdrop of the new millennium. To find a comparably arduous testing of personal relationships we would have to invoke the previous millennial dew, at the beginning of the 11th century, in the bowels of what we smugly refer to as the Dark Ages. In that period the quest for emotional commitment (as well as for bread) was constantly undermined by non-supportive world events; e.g., the assassination of Kenneth III in Scotland, the poisoning of Bloody Otto of the Holy Roman Empire, the ascent of the Seljukian Turks in Asia Minor and of the Fatamite caliphs in Egypt. It does not require a schematic mind to recognize similar pressures on embryonic 21st-century sensibilities from the fatal drug overdoses of popular music stars, the unhampered global expansion of fast food franchises, and the rise of religious fundamentalism from the caves of Afghanistan to the studios of the 700 Club.

But as tempting as it might be to suggest that the present crisis in human relations is merely the latest lava from an inevitable millennial eruption, such a conclusion would be more consoling than accurate. One elementary fact alone precludes all the analogies that might be drawn between the two epochs: PEOPLE OF ALL GENDERS HAVE LIVED ONE THOUSAND YEARS SINCE THE ELEVENTH CENTURY!!! Put another way, we are one thousand years older since Bloody Otto sampled the wrong dish, we have had a thousand more years of experiencing the traps of non-nurturing relationships, and we have spent 10 centuries more of potential solutions for maximizing the profitability of human interconnection and minimizing losses from failed investments. And with what result? Existential malaise. A sense of futility that we have tried everything and nothing works. Increasing gratuitousness as a response to the feeling of futility. Relentless violence as a companion to the gratuitousness. House and Senate committees investigating all the violence and endorsing the use of V-chips on television monitors. We aren't in a situation analogous to that of the 11th-century peasantry for the simple reason that, unlike us, it didn't squander 1,000 more years of opportunity for grasping our terrestrial misery. We are WORSE OFF.

If the growth of our corporeal and incorporeal needs has taught us anything by now, it is that misery not only loves company, it positively adores SYSTEMS. Across the centuries we have rushed to one deceptively organized corpus of thought after another in the vain search for clues to the dynamics of human behavior and to the appropriate governors for supplying the right mixture of JOY, HAPPINESS, and PROFIT. The two most venerable systems we have resorted to have been religious and philosophical. On a religious plane generations of forebears have been attracted to the theology, morality, and ritual offered by reverential practice, trusting it would deliver workable relationships in an afterworld as much as on this planet. Those of a more philosophical cast have sought explanations for their thoughts and feelings in arguments that, at their extreme, have proposed that there are no such things as thoughts and feelings in the first place. But while followers of both approaches have been numerous at every stage in history, triggering wars and disputes over academic copyrights, neither religion nor philosophy has ever encompassed the full range of human striving and its implications for emotional sharing, self-esteem, and fruitful career paths. To use their own vernaculars, religion has proved to be godless, philosophy to be mindless.

Aside from religion and philosophy, there have been a myriad of other tantalizing systems drafted for explicating human direction. Our most distant ancestors, for example, identified their characters with the animal life of the forest and plains. Although commonly confused with the earliest forms of religious exercise, this zoomorphic vision actually accorded a respect to the material and spiritual worlds that the average religion paid short shrift to in its preoccupation with confirming some transcendent entity abetting biochemical degeneration as the only desirable goal; i.e., if I'm 75 and have a brain tumor, I must be ready to meet my Maker. By contrast, the zoomorphic vision perceived in the annual behavioral cycles of the bear, the eagle, and the salmon the caprices and obligations of societal living; it posited mauling, screeching, and spawning as indispensable expressions of sharing. That many of these animals later underwent "conversion," becoming symbols even for chastity and contemplation, reflects the fear organized religion had regarding their competitive appeal to the typical woodsman.

But even before religions had tamed its contents, the zoo-morphic vision had revealed itself as an insufficient model for human interaction. Most obvious was the fact that animals *liked* being in a rut, and had little incentive for changing their ways. The ambivalences of cohabitation, the insecurities sparked by mysterious nightly prowls, the seasonality of sex drives, the lack of ambition beyond commanding a waterhole—none of these qualities promoted long-term human identification. In the end, anxiety for a systematic illumination had little to show for its pangs except meat, bones, and fur.

Other would-be ordinations from the animate world have been even less compelling. The humors of black bile, yellow bile, blood, and phlegm might have appeared comprehensive to some ancient Greeks, but not to many of their descendants, who had to wonder why success had to be synonymous with the viscous and disgusting. The Bodyists of 12th-century England had their moment in the outlook that human beings broke down into Nose, Chest, Elbow, Nate, and Foot types. While they would have a hovering influence again in the 20th century, the Bodyists failed to inspire for any great span of time the Yorkshireman who, on a good day, liked to believe he could derive pleasure and fulfillment from *all* his parts and who, on a bad day, watched *all* his parts being drawn and quartered. Equally unsuccessful, after fads of varying duration, were the 13th-century Barbers of Turkey with their emphasis on Canine, Molar, and Incisor personalities; the 14th-century Retinas of Samos with their divisions of the Green-Eyed, Blue-Eyed, and Brown-Eyed Trait Bearers; and the 15th-century Dominican Friars of Inquisition Spain who ranked men for honesty and purity by Ten Fingers, Nine Fingers, Three Fingers, and Stumps.

The inanimate world has been no more forthcoming, even when the physical sciences have been recruited for the effort. Thus, while alchemists from fifth-century China all the way up to 12th-century Europe were adept at characterizing metals by their potential for being transformed into gold or silver, their failure actually to achieve any such re-composition discouraged disciples who, as willing as they might have been to accept themselves as Lead or Tin types as a premise, found themselves having to abandon all real hope of moving upward to more lustrous self-images. That same kind of anti-climax has contributed to the more recent aversion to seizing upon the Atomic Table for emotional guidance; moreover, there has been an added suspicion since Hiroshima and Nagasaki that, however suggestively idiosyncratic a specific element might appear, its true Atomic Table value (and thus of the person identifying with it) could be measured solely by its capacity for being vital to a nuclear fallout. In a similar vein, attempts to align the struggles of human enterprise with the properties of precious stones have expired before chemical realities; to name merely one, how the outwardly versatile, affluent, and subtly majestic Opals Personality is prone to disintegrating and disappearing without warning.

In our own time, the social sciences have held out one archetypical system after another for gauging, comparing, and projecting human tendencies. For psychiatrists (with their obvious borrowings from the 12th-century Bodyists), we are inclined to be oral, anal, or genital in our affective priorities. For sociologists, we are traceable as white collar, blue collar, or police collar. For economists, we relate to one another as the employed, the underemployed, the unemployed, or the welfare cheat. Political scientists rate us Democratic Republicans, Republican Democrats, or Irrelevant. Television ratings researchers mark our tendencies as those of Network, Cable, or Dish. Opinion poll scholars compartmentalize us as Being Against Train Collisions, Being for Train Collisions, or Not Knowing What a Train Collision Is and Wanting to See One Before We Make Up Our Minds.

The social sciences systems have been as popular in our age as the religious and philosophical systems were to eons of incomplete people now completely dead. But just as with those abandoned forms of intellection, the social sciences systems have survived on mere familiarity long beyond their actual grip on the imagination. Anecdotal evidence alone indicates it has been decades since anyone outside a singles bar or AA meeting felt truly insightful about cataloging a date as oral, anal, or genital in tendency. To a great extent, in fact, it has been the very failure of the social sciences systems that has precipitated a critical phase in our present difficulties. Unlike the relationship-addicted at the end of the 19th century, say, when even critics of Freud's Id, Ego, and Superego personalities could still look forward to the demarcations being brewed by Jung, Adler, and Chopra, contemporary anxieties about our place in another's life and insurance coverage have little promise of rescue. We seem to have used up all the systems we have been capable of devising. We show increasing vulnerability to hot flashes, shortness of breath, and irritating allergies. We throb, we pant, and we scratch as if these physical responses alone will summon forth some new antidote for our ailment. With what consequence? At most, INFLAMMATION and INFECTION.

If there is one school of systematic projection that might appear to be unaffected by the present crisis, it is that postulating the daily influences of other worlds on our needs; that is to say, believers in the astrological sciences. Certainly, the zodiacalists have not been inhibited by the vacuities revealed over time by religion, philosophy, zoomorphism, bodyism, gemology, psychiatry, and sociology. On the contrary, it has been their assumption from the start that earth-inspired representations of a particular person's possible parameters for positive power provided, at best, a self-fulfilling prophecy. In their emphasis on emotional objectivity, zodiacalists have instead always looked skyward—to the orbs. If they have occasionally given the impression of accepting some of the oldest premises of religion (for instance, in their adoption of names tracing directly back to Greek theisms), and have also sometimes looked captive to the accidental sequences of calendars, they have equally demonstrated an openness in conceding the expediency of many of their constructs, acknowledging that their working hypotheses were eminently perfectible through further knowledge of the cosmos and its disparate parts. Thus, astrological adepts have eschewed dogmatism, recognizing that Hindus, Hebrews, and Chinese have different healing and bonanza schedules with the sky than do, say, Bulgarians and Comanches. They have also rejected simplistic conclusions that would equate an individual destiny with birth dates, birth hours, or birth minutes. In their elaborately plotted conjunctions of cosmic phenomena and human self-assertion, zodiacalists have indeed ultimately argued that anything can happen to anybody at any time. If that insight has struck critics as too indiscriminate for personality analysis and tactical application, it has impressed its own adherents for its tolerance of planetary and extra-planetary developments.

But that said, the zodiacalists have also had problems of their own of late, making them as vulnerable to the current crisis as any other group. One problem has stemmed from accelerating immigration patterns, leading to a growing confusion in our great metropolitan centers about the most relevant calendars and astral houses; e.g., the Year of the Dragon in one neighborhood is celebrated as the Year of the Panther only a few blocks away. On top of that, dissidents within the astrological science community have been stepping up efforts to have some pet sign, celestial movement, or stellar influence dominate charts, in effect demanding a total reinterpretation of mankind's traditional relationship with the cosmos. And even these rebels have been a minor headache compared to fragmented but best-selling Yahoo cults that would dispense with the entire solar system in favor of identifying the complexities of human need and succor with a salvageable planet or two (e.g., Mars and Venus). Spurred on by the material success of the Yahoos, astronomers have begun claiming discoveries of new orbs and even new non-existent orbs known as black holes with no fixed place in established horoscopy. The upshot has been interpretative anarchy, waning faith in the stability of the heavens, and a suppurating cynicism among former disciples that has reduced astrology to just another bankrupt social science.

It has been against this background of overwhelming negative energies that Dr. Alan Gibb, most notably but not exclusively in his milestone work *You're a Peewee, I'm a Bambino*, has stepped forward with a revolutionary proposal for seizing, directing, and profiting from the human process.

1

FRANCHISEMENT

We had lost that team feeling about life.
We were feeling disenfranchised.

R. ALAN GIBB is not an easy person to know. This is ironic insofar as nobody in recent history has enabled us to know ourselves more than the wan rail of a man who is seldom without a tube of Jolly Rancher candies in one hand and the wrappings from those he has already sucked in the other. Pleasure and waste go literally hand in hand with him, and the mind between his appendages is an enigma. True to character, he prefers it that way. An interview with Dr. Alan Gibb, he makes clear immediately, is not an interview about Dr. Alan Gibb, it is an interview about Franchisement.

Another thing Gibb makes clear at once (apparently on the advice of his attorney) is that he never discovered the name of the 10-year-old boy who inspired his Franchisement vision on a summer afternoon in 1991. This has enkindled ambivalent feelings in him ever since. As he puts it:

> If I'd asked his name and then used it in some article, I might've gotten into some Hollywood kind of thing. You know, the lunatic father of a brat actor coming around to extort millions in his

son's name. From that point of view, thank Christ, I never knew his name. But on the other hand, I like to know things.

Gibb's fateful encounter took place at the Manhattan intersection of Broadway and West 76th Street shortly after two o'clock on the afternoon of July 16, 1991. The professor had gone to the corner to wait for the bus that would take him uptown to his scheduled 3:00 class at Columbia University. At the time, he was a 52-year-old member of Columbia's prestigious Psychology Department, specializing in Omissive Language (the words and phrases that never quite make it to the tongue in conversation because of extraordinary mutual understanding, censored annoyance, or tact). The New York native recalls staring through the boy at the bus stop while his thoughts wandered over the lecture he was slated to give on such normally omitted conversational phrases as "I could've told you that a long time ago" and "Why do you think I want to listen to this shit?" Gibb:

> Then I blinked and took in the kid. He was making a big fuss with his mother about not wanting to visit some friend of hers uptown. Then in the next breath he was asking if his mother's friend still had her dog. If she still had her dog, that was okay, he said, because he liked the dog and the ice cream she always gave him and the way she always let him watch her cable stations. It was a pretty incoherent tirade. The mother, she pretended she didn't hear all his babbling. She just kept looking to see if the bus was coming.

Then Gibb noticed something else about the boy.

> It was the way he was dressed. He had a pair of shorts with the Mets insignia, his T-shirt said Boston Red Sox, and his cap was from the Yankees. He had apparently been to every giveaway day in a baseball stadium on the east coast. I recall mulling whether that might not create an identity problem for him. Then and there, though, I didn't realize that such a passing thought would become the cornerstone of Franchisement thinking.

GENERAL THEORY

Unlike other systematic approaches to typifying and projecting the directions of human empowerment, Franchisement calls for no special knowledge or industry on the part of its adherents. Despite its obvious figurative debts to baseball, practitioners are NEITHER EXPECTED NOR ENCOURAGED to acquaint themselves with the national pastime; quite the contrary, the assumption is that, even when in need of positive reinforcement, they will simply consult the writings of Dr. Alan Gibb and other Franchisement thinkers, purchase what they require, then forget about their crisis until another intervention becomes imperative. As Dr. Sidney Willinger of the University of Indiana's Leisure Sciences Department explains:

> One problem with some of the other systems before
> Franchisement was that you had to keep a lot in your head.
> People were always going around saying they were Platonists or
> Aristotelians, for instance, without knowing the actual difference
> because they hadn't read either one since college. Franchisement
> demands none of that kind of memory. You draft your identity
> from existing possibilities, you read over your assets, liabilities,
> and tendencies, and there you have it. The only thing you have to
> remember is who you want to be. If you can't manage that, you
> belong in a jar anyway.

Although Willinger might have been overstating the case, there is little question that one of Franchisement's strongest appeals is that it is SIMPLE. And that has never been an accident.

Days after his encounter at the bus stop, Gibb was still pasting together the fragments from the experience to see what they revealed. After some of his most difficult noodling since pioneering the study of omissive language, he isolated four principal elements from the event:

1. The child's multi-directed, even contradictorily directed, passions.
2. The confusion of baseball apparel on the boy's person.

3. The indifference of the mother to the boy's confusion.
4. The fact that the encounter took place at West 76th Street—suggestive not only of the year of the establishment of the United States of America (1776), but also of the date of the first major league baseball game (1876).

Gibb:

To this day I remain convinced that if I had come upon an old man or a hooker at that stop, or come upon a kid with only a Boston T-shirt, or walked up to the next bus stop at 79th Street, Franchisement would not have happened. It was a commingling of events—a centering of omens, if you will—that made each of the individual elements vital to the determination of the experience.

Gibb's first insight was that there was a direct connection between the confusing verbal expressions of the 10-year-old's desires and the confusing apparel statements of his team loyalties, that he had been face to face with a bizarre illustration of the admonition that clothes can make the man. Equally important, according to the psychologist, were the specific contents of the two confusions:

Here's a 10-year-old who's going to be parked for the afternoon in front of a living room TV set, so his mother and her friend can sit out in the kitchen complaining about their careers and love lives. The boy is actually being told to WATCH THE GAME, and if he does, he will be rewarded with an ice cream. The dog of the mother's friend acts as something of a security guard, there to make sure the kid doesn't leave the TV set and intrude upon the REAL LIFE going on in the kitchen. Clearly, he was familiar with both the routine (thus his protest at the bus stop) and the compensations (thus his joyous anticipation of the dog, the cable channels, and the ice cream).

And the clothing?

Mind you, he wasn't wearing the insignias of just any three major league baseball teams. The logos represented the three teams with more passionate rancor among them than any others still east of the Mississippi. On an inter-relational level, the Yankees and Red Sox are a byword for estrangement. Then you have the Mets, with their plague-on-both-your-houses view of the others. The worst kind of emotional violence was running all over that wretched boy's body!

Where other trained professionals might have stopped at that analysis, Gibb pushed on to speculations seminal for the growth of Franchisement. Even years after the fact, he can relish the next step with the same gusto he customarily shows for popping a Jolly Rancher into his mouth.

First, I hypothesized what the child's behavior might have been if he had been wearing only his Yankees paraphernalia. I concluded there would have been nothing in his skull but the gaudy profit he anticipated—the cable TV, ice cream, and dog. He would have deluded himself into thinking the outing was at his initiative, and most likely would have asked why his mother didn't hail a cab instead of waiting for a bus in a neighborhood in need of a healthy dose of public funding to gain respectability.

Then I pictured him wearing only his Red Sox shirt. Mind you, this was back before Boston hadn't won anything but first prize in excuses for why they always lost. That kid, I thought, wouldn't do anything but whine at the bus stop about how unfair life was. He would sulk so much he'd persuade himself even his ostensible gains—the TV, dog, and ice cream—were punishments waiting to happen. Maybe the TV would electrocute him, the dog bite him, the ice cream give him food poisoning. He'd be inconsolable, and insist that was his fate.

If he'd been wearing only the Mets shorts? He would figure he was going to spend the greatest afternoon any kid ever had. He'd be woefully cocky, curse the bus for taking so long to take

him to the scene of his instant gratification. As soon as he
arrived, though, the dog would run away from him, the ice cream
would drip over his clothes, and the only thing on TV would be a
black-and-white Joan Crawford movie that would scare the hell
out of him.

Such projections, of course, were Franchisement at its most rudi-
mentary. Nevertheless, Gibb's intuition that the full range of human
resourcefulness and folly might correspond in an illuminating way
to a baseball franchise characterology already marked a significant
step forward from earlier, pupal glimmerings of the kind.

PRECEDENTS

Undoubtedly, Franchisement's most noted ideological predecessor
had been the worldview that the universe was divisible into
Winners and Losers. A perspective popularized by the Union Army
and directed against the Confederacy in the aftermath of the Civil
War (1861-65), Winners and Losers had then fallen into disuse for
several decades following the embarrassments of the massacre at
Little Big Horn and the various slaughters of American troops in
France in World War I. Only in the 1920s had it once again become
a cynosure for peer perceptions—within the specific context of those
who felt (arrogantly) empowered by being followers of the Murderers
Row Yankees, as opposed to those who (wretchedly) sought empathy
with one of the other seven teams then in the American League. But
that revival hadn't lasted long, and justly so according to Jennifer
Pryor, dean of the Harvard School of Theoretical Business:

> Winners and Losers was really the equivalent of saying you could
> only be Aries or Gemini, Pluto or Neptune, man or woman. It
> totally ignored the diversification impulse, leaving millions of
> people to wonder why, even as Yankee fans, they felt like losers
> and millions more to ask themselves why, despite being rabid
> about the St. Louis Browns, they felt like winners. It was a
> troubling paradox.

An almost identical emotional disillusion had awaited those in the 1930s who had identified their needs and lacks with feelings of being Major League or Minor League personalities. Pryor, again:

> You had a lot of people in cities like Chicago and Philadelphia who were supposed to feel major league in their affective relationships, but who were actually under enormous stress from an inability to acquit a task as simple as taking out the garbage. There was an equally significant number of people in places like Ames or Wilkes-Barre who were supposed to be minor league personalities, but who were in fact raking it in hand over fist by gambling against the stock market, investing in Hitler and Mussolini, or just enjoying warm, vibrant relationships in their huts. Something did not scan in the major-minor league distinction.

Gibb agreed. The more he sorted out the particles of Franchisement's predecessors, the more he knew he was venturing into uncharted territory. And that wasn't his only surprise. Given the scarcity of Franchisement-type endeavors prior to his own, he was also astounded to find that the first major impediment to formulating a coherent, reflective system of human resonance was an *overabundance* of organized psychognomies.

> There was simply too much dilution of character signs. A Florida Marlins *and* Tampa Bay Ray Personality? It was as if a zodiacalist had 24 months instead of 12 at his disposal, so had to delve into how many scorpions also had two faces or liked to tote water.

Moreover, Gibb realized, he had more than the contemporary big-league franchises to deal with. His potential market also included people who still identified with franchises that no longer existed; for instance, the Brooklyn Dodgers, Milwaukee Braves, and any number of manifestations of the Baltimore Orioles going back to the 1880s. He could not help feeling this problem acutely since he thought of himself as part of such a list. As he told the monthly *Washingtonian* in June 1997:]

I've always considered myself a Washington Senators Personality.
With my bent for nostalgia and positive thinking, I have never
accepted the gibberish about Washington being "first in war, first
in peace, and last in the American League." Call me Pollyanna,
but I seem to remember that Washington came in about third
after China and North Korea in the Korean War, went out of its
way to stir the shit in the Middle East and Germany in the 1950s,
and usually finished ahead of the St. Louis Browns.

With his own mindset impacting his research, Gibb came across
more than 120 major league franchises since 1876 with claims
to distinct character and model applicability. "It goes without
saying," he said to an interviewer anyway, "that this would have
been an impossible task. It would be like a Bodyist insisting on an
individual personology for every finger on your hand, every tooth in
your mouth, and every hair on your ass. Yes, you want to guide the
customer into particularization, but you don't want to dissect him
into pulverization. Choices had to be made."

Thus was born Franchisement's Personal Standings League of
16 club types. There would seem little question that this particular
number was fed by the fact that 16 major clubs existed when Alan
Gibb was born into the world. And, of course, the fateful encounter
on West 76th Street took place on July 16. But over and above
these happy conjunctions, Gibb was able to satisfy himself that
with his 16 selections he had circled the bases of all primary human
endeavor. As he told an HBO interviewer:

The naysayers carp there should be 19 or 38 or 101 franchise
models. That's the same mob that wants Campbell's to market
oxtail turkey lentil soup. The human comedy degenerates to
farce if you throw anything at all on the shelf just to appease the
grousers.

2

A LEAGUE OF OUR OWN

S THE ONLY son of a luggage salesman and a public-school custodian, Dr. Alan Gibb has never apologized for his commercial acumen. He has even admitted for the record that he was lured initially to psychology by a *Wall Street Journal* survey indicating that profession as the most lucrative for members of his race, generation, and level of imagination. Thus, when it came to choose the 16 teams that would make up Franchisement's Personal Standings League, he did not hesitate to select those associated with the largest commercial markets. Fortunately, he discovered, these clubs corresponded to models for the broadest range of human aspiration, enterprise, and inadequacy.

What they also corresponded to were 16 of the most influential people in the professor's own life. Although he has played down this coincidence as not at all as important as the date of his epiphany at the bus stop and the number of teams existing when he was born, he did at least on one occasion rebuke a *Time* reporter for insinuating that nobody has ever had as many as 16 influential people in their lives. "I see no reason for your skepticism," Gibb told the newsman. "Maybe I've been luckier than most, maybe you've been unluckier than most. But I would suggest you go home tonight and really count the people who have influenced you. Something tells me you'll discover it's a longer list than your parents, the woman you lost your virginity with, an old algebra teacher, and Henry Luce."

The normally tranquil Gibb's snappishness with the *Time* reporter points to the doubts that greeted his Personal Standings League selections. He also had to defend his inclusion of three defunct franchises—the Brooklyn Dodgers, New York Giants, and Washington Senators. On the first two, he told NBC's *Today* show:

> There are plenty of old people in the United States of America. How do you make a profit if you write off California, Florida, and Arizona? On the other hand, I didn't want to look like I was catering to the nursing home crowd, either. No doubt you got lots of old manic depressives in thrall even to this day to the Kansas City Athletics. But they don't have the demographics behind them the old Dodger and Giant fans have.
>
> They say New York is where it's at? Well, it's also where it *was* at.

And the Senators that left Washington for Minnesota in 1960?

> Washington is Washington. People like to remember what they once believed in even if they never really believed in it, and I'm unable to think of a stronger point of reference for that characteristic than D.C.

Given Gibb's premises, the other 13 teams were more predictable: the New York Mets, New York Yankees, Boston Red Sox, Philadelphia Phillies, Atlanta Braves, Cleveland Indians, Cincinnati Reds, Chicago Cubs, St. Louis Cardinals, Houston Astros, Arizona Diamondbacks, Los Angeles Dodgers, and San Francisco Giants. Fans of the Chicago White Sox were particularly aggravated that their team had been left off the typology chart. "I always remind them that's the second team in the Second City," Gibb can chuckle, producing another tube of Jolly Ranchers from his brocaded cowboy shirt pocket. "You want to identify with that, I tell them, you already know enough about yourself not to need me. That always pisses them off even more."

Joel Sternheim, associate professor of infomercials at Miami State Business School, endorses Gibb's final selections. Sternheim:

> You can't please everybody all the time. It's usually a waste of time even trying to please some of them every once in a while. If you're not going to prioritize, you're going to end up out of business *a priore*.

Father Benjamin Acocella, S.J., president of the Ecumenical Council on Mental Observances, seconds Sternheim. Acocella:

> You can go on forever arguing about the number of angels on the head of a pin. Yahweh and Allah know that I have. But that's never really been the theological point of that debate. The main thing is that Franchisement has given us another pin.

To his credit, Gibb wasn't so easily flattered. Just because he had settled on the 16 teams that would make up his Personal Standings League and just because he had retorts for his critics, he realized, didn't mean customers would come flocking to his 900 numbers, books, and videos. Most immediately, there was the danger that the Personal Standings League would create misunderstandings about its targeted audience; i.e., convey the impression it was only for and about baseball addicts. As he put it in his best-selling *You're a Peewee, I'm a Bambino*:

> The jock vision was bad enough, but then you had the Rand-McNally Syndrome on top of it. For too long this society has put exaggerated value on geographical emotion. You go to one of those afternoon TV shows on a freebie, the emcee picks you out of the audience and asks where you're from, you tell him, and everyone claps, like you deserve credit for where your parents got laid. You try to make time with a single in a bar, she asks where you're from, you tell her, and suddenly she acts like she's got some vital clue to you. What I had to get across to my customers

was that a guy from Chicago wasn't necessarily a Chicago Cubs Personality because he rooted for them. I'd never spent a day in Washington until being invited to the White House, but that has not prevented me from being a Washington Senators Personality my whole life. There are Estonians getting off the boat today who've never heard of baseball, but they could still be Arizona Diamondback Personalities. The nut I had to crack was to divorce Franchisement not just from baseball, but also from its narrow reliance on a geographical bias. In a way, I had to question the very foundations of pastime and place.

If the extent of the Franchisement empire today attests to how masterfully he has met the challenge, it also invites forgetfulness of the arduous journey Alan Gibb had to undertake to travel beyond geographical emotionalism and other obstacles in the way of his ULTIMATE SUCCESS. As he has sighed on more than one occasion: "Lewis and Clark had guides, canoes, and girlfriends. I had none of those things."

3

THE JOURNEY

BROOKLYN DODGERS   (Mascot: Fred Gibb)

Although he didn't know it at the time, Alan Gibb set off on his
journey toward Franchisement when his father, Fred Gibb, a
traveling salesman for Samsonite luggage and leather goods, took
him to his first baseball game—at Ebbets Field in Brooklyn, to see
the Dodgers playing the Phillies. Two hours after watching the final
out of a Dodger victory, then eleven-year-old Alan was informed by
his mother that his father hadn't dropped him back at the house
before going around to Strohmeyer's deli for a half-pound of bologna,
but had in fact taken off for parts unknown forever. In denying the
finality of his father's departure for his own peace of mind, Alan
kept returning to the curious idea of a luggage salesman being on
the lam. Was that appropriate or merely redundant? Did it mean
his father was the victim of some insidious occupational hazard
and wasn't really responsible for his decision to take off, or did it
mean his father had been packing his bags and bags and bags for
his flight long before announcing it to his mother?

While trying to make up his mind on this point, Alan clung to
his last images of Fred Gibb—his father getting into an argument

with a scorecard vendor, his father telling him he could have a hot dog only if he didn't get mustard on his shirt, and his father leaving Ebbets Field with a grunt that the Dodgers had finally won one. For Alan, the Dodgers became the home fire he tendered for the night (he was sure it would come) the luggage salesman finally gave up the road and returned to the hearth. He saved every penny he could to buy bleacher seats for weekend games, and when he didn't have enough money for a ticket, he stood outside the gates of the ballpark before a game anyway, confident his street urchin pose would net him an extra ticket or spare quarter. Once inside Ebbets Field, he continually scanned the other faces in the bleachers in the hope he would spot his father and be able to voice the monologue he had been practicing in his head for talking Fred Gibb into accompanying him back home after the game. His backup plan was keeping score of the games assiduously, envisioning the day he would be able to greet his returned father with a complete record of everything they had missed seeing together. To the same end, he refused to eat bologna until he could dig into the half-pound his father brought back from Strohmeyer's.

The day of return never came. Instead, the Dodgers also went— to Los Angeles. Once again, Alan Gibb found himself before a conundrum: Did the defection of the Dodgers to California constitute another betrayal of his affections or were they merely living up to their nickname as elusive objects of love? Once again, the curious triumphed over the clear.

NEW YORK GIANTS   *Mascot: Louise Gibb*

Whatever other stresses her husband's departure had caused, Louise Gibb did not suffer financially. As the third highest-paid public-school custodian in New York City, she was even able to reassure Alan that "we're better off now—we have only two mouths to feed on my money." Alan took this bravado to mean that selling Samsonite luggage door-to-door was not what it was cracked up to be—another small shock insofar as his mother seemed to have spent most days at home, at most going off to her job at P.S. 9

a couple of hours twice a week. Indeed, the belated realization that she had been making more money talking to her neighbors at the kitchen table than his father had earned dragging suitcases from apartment to apartment in the middle of the worst summer heat and winter snow, so stunned him that he briefly harbored an ambition to become a school custodian himself.

Then there was his mother's reaction to his passion for the Dodgers. When she wasn't scolding him for wasting his money on bleacher seats and pennants and stickpin photos of the players, she was slipping in salty reminders that Fred Gibb had been a Dodger fan and "see where that got us." Alan fended off these jabs with all the good humor at his disposal; at bottom, he told himself, it was only his mother's way of saying she was as lonely without his father as he was. But then one afternoon he returned home from school to find Louise hosting a TV party for another custodian named Bobby Irvin, a towering man with a mustache, shaved head, and biceps straining under his shirt. The two of them were on the couch in front of the black-and-white Admiral, and the set was turned to a game between the New York Giants and Pittsburgh Pirates. Alan was perplexed to see his mother drinking scotch in the afternoon, and altogether dumbfounded when she laughed at him and said she and Bobby Irvin had been watching "really good teams, not your Dodgers." Bobby Irvin laughed, too, then took his hand off the back of the couch near Louise's hair and ran his stubby cigar of a finger through his mustache, the way silent movie villains did.

Alan was confused. He didn't bother correcting his mother that the Giants were seventh and the Pirates eighth in an eight-team league while the Dodgers were first. On the other hand, he liked the idea she had advanced beyond her stated aversion to baseball to endorse a specific team, even the hateful Giants. But on the third hand, he heard too much embarrassment in her voice—the kind he associated with the guilt of school custodians about staying home to screw while lessons were going on in all the classrooms. In the end, he wished she hadn't said anything, and was glad when the two of them didn't insist he accompany them around the corner to the Chinese restaurant. He didn't mind a couple of years later, either, when the Giants went off to San Francisco. As badly as he had wanted the Dodgers to stay, it struck him as appropriate that they have the Giants for company on the road to California.

NEW YORK YANKEES   (Mascot: Archie Geis)

Alan thought of his early teenage years as penal isolation: Knowing nobody he considered his equal on such subjects as the Dodgers and Bobby Irvin, he spent a lot of time playing with himself. At that, these were his least oppressive moments. First, there was his mother's endless ranting about what she called a "new element" at her school; no matter how much they paid, as he overheard her saying once on the phone, she was "never going to clean up after sambos." She made good on that vow, too, reducing her already minimal hours at P.S. 9 and somehow winning a series of raises and citations of merit for doing little more than telling callers where they could find some key or fuse box. With Louise around the house so much, Alan lacked incentive even for cutting his classes.

Then there was Archie Geis, a General Motors showroom salesman Louise doted on as openly as she had been coy about Bobby Irvin. It was trying enough for Alan to contend with Archie Geis's blue stripe suits, patriotic sermons, and stupid jokes that always had the sound of having been memorized exclusively for him. Worse were his mother's leading questions about his opinion of Archie—a regular exercise he usually rejected with noncommittal grunts, but also with a growing uneasiness that he was being asked to own up to what everybody else had already accepted as reality. By the afternoon he finally allowed as how Archie was "okay," it felt like his last chance to be invited to the wedding.

Archie Geis the stepfather had fewer jokes but more cars. Once a month he arrived home with some new GM model he hadn't moved out of his showroom. Cadillacs, Buicks, Oldsmobiles, Pontiacs—he found nothing amiss in rotating them for a few weeks of personal use before returning them to the store. When even Louise wondered over supper one evening if such borrowings didn't belie the showroom's claims of selling only unused vehicles, Archie observed that as long as he was in the driver's seat he would take whatever he wanted and she should shut up. What covered it all for him was his favorite boast that "you drive a GM, it's like you're using pipes from U.S. Steel or playing for the Yankees."

If Alan sometimes envied Archie's cavalier approach to automotives, he was never short on resentment of the man, either, and never more so than when Archie insisted on teaching him how to drive. He didn't want Archie Geis teaching him anything, especially in a stolen car. The more he had to hear about the benefits of power steering and layaway payment plans during their Saturday morning lessons, the more he knew he would never be comfortable confronting the congested roads of life with such arrogance. GM cars weren't just alien to him, they were evil incarnate, and it felt like a victory of sorts when Archie finally gave up trying to teach him how to drive. (He also came to despise heavy machinery on the premise that it involved U.S. Steel products.)

PHILADELPHIA PHILLIES   (Mascot: Teddy Doofle)

Alan sat apprehensively one afternoon in the waiting room of Dr. Amos Rosenberg, D.D.S. Then Teddy Doofle started telling him that the root canal work awaiting him was nothing, that he, Teddy, had lost three teeth in one sitting to Rosenberg and it hadn't hurt in the least. Although Alan hadn't known Doofle previously except as a neighborhood kid who went to a different school, he was moved to the thought of tracking down the bastard and yanking out the rest of his teeth after staggering home from his session with Rosenberg. Not only had the dentist hurt him with needles, drills, and wires, he had acted positively outraged to have so much writhing slowing down his sadistic task.

Teddy Doofle? When Alan finally cornered the liar in Sam's candy store two days later, Doofle just shrugged and said he thought Alan would have worried less if he hadn't known what was coming. Alan was so disarmed by the explanation that he ended up walking home with Doofle, talking about this and that. A few days later, he was invited to the Doofle apartment for supper, after which he, Teddy, and Mr. Doofle turned on a Phillies game that was being shown for New York fans starved by the departure of the Dodgers and Giants. Mr. Doofle said the Phillies were rotten, Alan recalled they had been the losing team the day he had last seen his father, and Teddy said it must have been tough to think about that every time Philadelphia lost because, god knew, they lost a lot. Mr. Doofle said beggars couldn't be choosers when it came to National League ball in New York. When Teddy chimed in that he would rather watch the Phillies play anybody than watch the American League Yankees, Alan felt a glow of excitement at having found the closest thing to a brother he had ever found. Before going home that evening, he shared with Teddy all his conflicts with his mother and Archie Geis, unable to remember when he had felt so free.

But then one night a week later, Mr. Doofle rolled home plastered from his job at the neighborhood library branch, picked up a hammer and whacked both Mrs. Doofle and Teddy to death in their beds, then went up to the roof of his building and jumped off. The official verdict was summarized in a *Daily News* headline as DOOFLE CRACKED. Alan wanted to go to the funeral, but it was held somewhere in New Jersey with Mrs. Doofle's family, and Archie said that would have been too long a trip even for the fleet of GM cars at his command.

BOSTON RED SOX   (Mascot: Gloria Tavarez)

Alan met Gloria Tavarez in his junior year at high school. She came from Puerto Rico, and he liked the way she gave the finger to Richie Burke on her very first day for calling her a spic. When he ended up partnered with her in reading aloud *Romeo and Juliet* in English class a week later, he fell in love with her. Better, she fell in love with him when he deliberately stopped reading his lines until Richie Burke and his cronies in the back row put an end to their sniggering. They started eating lunch together in the cafeteria, where she told him about the tiny lizards that ran over supper tables in San Juan to drive away the bugs and he told her how his father, the Dodgers, the Giants, and Teddy Doofle had left New York. Walking her to the subway for her trip home every afternoon, he also heard about the various sentiments in Puerto Rico for continued territorialism, statehood, and independence; he in turn filled in Gloria on the way his mother seemed to be screwing the Board of Education with her no-show job and Archie seemed to be screwing GM customers with his driven cars. She thought that kind of thing was worldwide, but for his part he couldn't think of any other place on earth where remaining a territory, accepting full statehood, or gaining national independence were hotly debated alternatives. She said she liked him, he hadn't thought it necessary to say he liked her.

Alan kissed Gloria Tavarez at the beginning of an Anthony Perkins movie, she initiated a kiss of her own near the end of it. He went to his first school dance with her, and couldn't believe he was entering the auditorium with somebody with her lilac perfume, neat black dress, and full calves. He liked the feeling of having so many eyes on their backs, and even more how so many teachers came over to congratulate him for emerging from his shell and Gloria for finding a friend so fast in her new mainland surroundings. What he liked less was Gloria's edginess going home on the subway that night—what he finally got her to confess was a despondency for having been singled out at the dance. "We're losers, Alan," she blurted out as the train pulled into her stop. "That's what those people really meant by calling us winners."

Dismayed as he was before such bleakness, Alan nevertheless had Gloria laughing by the time they had walked the four blocks to her two-family home. Every dumb joke Archie Geis had told him sprang to mind, and before her toothy smiles acquire a humor he hadn't appreciated in them before. Even with the lights on in the windows above them, they stood in the alleyway next to her side door necking more thrillingly than they ever had for close to an hour. He felt adventurous, he felt adult, he felt in love with Destiny itself. When she finally snapped her bra closed again under her dress and quietly opened the side door to go upstairs, he felt blessed by everybody—by his teachers, by Archie Geis, by anybody he had ever passed in the street who had given him a look hinting he would never amount to anything.

His euphoria lasted only a couple of more dates. Gloria didn't want him going under her pants, she began hanging out with girls who in turn drew her closer to Richie Burke's circle, and his mother thought Puerto Ricans should take the independence option and stay out of New York. A month later there was another school dance, and Gloria attended it with Larry Holman while Alan stayed home watching "Dragnet" with Archie Geis. It took some time before he became objective enough about his hurt to accept that he had never been meant to go all the way with Gloria Tavarez, that (as she had said on the subway) they were born losers who would only suffer needlessly by entertaining illusions they were otherwise.

WASHINGTON SENATORS   (Mascot: Walter Luderus)

Alan persuaded his mother to pay for a three-day class trip to Washington. He had no particular desire to see the White House or the Capitol, but he was determined to go as soon as he heard the itinerary included a visit to FBI headquarters. All the way down to Washington on the train, while his classmates whooped and hollered around him, he pictured himself shaking hands with an FBI agent and sharing some troubling confidences. There was Gloria Tavarez, of course, with her dubious residential status in New York. There was his stepfather Archie Geis, who must have been guilty of some interstate larceny in using GM cars shipped from Michigan for personal purposes. There was even his mother, who appeared to be part of a citywide featherbedding scheme that the New York City police were abetting through inaction. He couldn't see himself going so far as to make specific accusations, but he did want some answers about all the shadiness going on around him from somebody in knowing authority.

The agent who conducted the tour of the FBI's historical archives, fingerprints division, and other departments was Walter Luderus, an emaciated man in a smelly brown suit who seemed to grimace in pain every time he opened his mouth. Alan found the opportunity to talk to him as they were walking down a dark basement hall after seeing the shooting ranges. While the rest of the class dawdled over showcases filled with plaques and trophies, Alan sidled up to Luderus to wonder aloud about how busy Puerto Ricans had been keeping the FBI. As he had been doing throughout the tour, Luderus set his jaw painstakingly, then said: "Too bad they're not Cubans. Then the Senators could sign 'em cheap, put them in uniform, and we'd always know where they are."

It took Alan a moment to realize Luderus was making a joke, then an entire afternoon of wandering from the Washington Monument to the Jefferson Memorial to accept that the agent had somehow read his thoughts. However objective he claimed to be about Gloria Tavarez's drift away from him, he finally grasped, he had remained possessive about her, didn't want her on her own at all, wanted her to realize she belonged to him. He wanted to know what she was doing with Larry Holman, right down to the smallest detail of how far she was letting Holman go under her panties in the alley next to her house. If only she had been in a uniform and out on a field in front of thousands of people all the time, he wouldn't have had to guess. And what about the stories she was telling Holman and her new friends about *him*? If she hadn't spoken English so fluently, she wouldn't have been able to tell them anything. Luderus was absolutely right: It *was* too bad she wasn't a Cuban instead of a Puerto Rican. At least Cubans admitted they were foreigners from the start, no whining about territories or states. Going home on the train, Alan was overwhelmed by how achingly he wanted everybody in his life—his mother and Archie Geis as much as Gloria Tavarez— to be a foreigner.

4

PITS

N HIS EFFORTS to divorce Franchisement theory from baseball's reliance on geographical prejudices, Dr. Alan Gibb was able to borrow from the experiences of earlier forms of systematic identification. He regarded the zodiacalists as especially instructive in this area:

It occurred to me that my Personal Standings League couldn't have been too different from the first steps taken by those horoscope guys. They had their 12 signs, they had worked it out along general lines how a Leo could be distinguished from a Capricorn. But so what? "I'm a lion and you're a goat, so now let's get on with life?" The pioneer horoscopists were shrewder than that. There was no percentage in anything so elementary. So what they did was complicate everything with all that cusp and ascending house stuff. I might start out by being a goat, but by the time all the subtleties were laid on top of that, I was also a lion, a bull, a crab, and a flounder. I'd become a goddamn zoo!

Indiana University's Sidney Willinger argues that Gibb's awareness on this point was as vital to the development of Franchisement as his earlier insights. Willinger:

We all say we like simplicity. But the simpler a phenomenon, the more we distrust it. In my own field of leisure studies, I've encountered this dynamic over and over again. A remote panel makes it easier to surf TV channels on the couch, but before you know it we've got zappers with more buttons on them than the dashboard of a 747. Automatic steering for our cars? Fabulous. But to make up for all that missing clutch work we add buzzers and lasers and electronic maps the U.S. Air Force could use to take out the Satan of the Month. What Alan grasped was that simplicity makes for a void and that it's the nature of the leisure animal to fill up that void as quickly as he can.

In short, Franchisement had to be more than SIMPLE; it also had to be extremely COMPLICATED.

But there was more to it than playing to the expectations of the man at rest. Gibb also had personal reasons for layering his Personal Standings League with the intricate and the pernickety. The closest he came to admit this was in a conversation with David Letterman during the national tour for his book *You're a Peewee, I'm a Bambino.* Asked by the CBS host what he thought of human beings, Gibb blurted: "I hate them."

Despite the predictable laughter he received from Letterman's audience, Gibb wasn't joking. Over the years, he has dodged accusations of misanthropy with a benevolent chuckle more translatable as confirmation than as a no-comment. This is nowhere clearer than in the basic typology he has assigned to the 16 personalities demarcated in the Personal Standings League. The Father of Franchisement's dour view of humanity emerges with dazzling lucidity in such attributes as *dissembling, dissipated, deceptive, destructive, dumb, degenerate, dim, dippy,* and any number of other *d* words. But as Gibb knew only too well, so much negativity was hardly geared toward popularizing Franchisement in the marketplace. Even though he was certain his potential customers shared his embittered outlook in their brains, he was equally sure they would never admit it for public consumption, would indeed strike the usual poses about the power of positive thinking, effectively aborting his business before it got off the ground.

Thus, he decided, his complication tool had to be powerful enough to counter the balefulness of his misanthropy, as implicit in the Personal Standings League typologies. It had to introduce elements of interpretation that completely reconditioned the tendencies of initial characterologies, thereby opening Franchisement to the mass audience it would not reach otherwise.

The solution turned out to be what Gibb has termed the Positional Identity Trait Sign, or PITS. And here again he acknowledges a debt to forerunners in the systematic thought market:

> All those horoscope loons had their familiar signs and pictures. The same thing with religions—all those crosses, crescents, Stars of David. If there has ever been a system in the world that didn't have a design element for reinforcing the message, I've never heard of it. One picture has always been worth a million bucks.

For Franchisement Gibb worked out five appropriate subdivisions for the triple aim of blunting his misanthropy, particularizing characterologies, and making his system more complicated. These five PITS of personality tendencies have been broken down as:

1. HITTING (symbol—baseball bat). Aggressive; usually self-absorbed, but capable of sacrifices; humorless; not especially bright; neurotic; ill-tempered.

2. PITCHING (symbol—human arm). Aggressive; committed to group success over individual achievement, but only if playing the lead role in attaining that objective; intelligent; glib; slow to anger but hard to appease; self-satisfied.

3. FIELDING (symbol—baseball glove). Defensive; guilt-laden; tries to be ingratiating; capable of sterling achievements; intelligent about his job but not much else; antic humor; eager for physical confrontation.

4. RUNNING (symbol—human leg). Irresponsible, often stupid; adventurous; health-conscious; indifferent to others; greedy; slick.

5. RAINCHECK (symbol—human tears). Indecisive; evasive; arbitrary; easily bored; banks on ulterior purposes.

For infomercials expert Joel Sternheim, the PITS fulfills the same dynamic in Franchisement that the antithesis plays in classic Hegelianism and Marxism. Sternheim:

> PITS is more than a corrective to simplicity. I would venture to say it is the vehicle within the Franchisement process for testing all imposed reality. If the Personal Standings League can't stand up to the testing it brings, there can be no ultimate synthesis. Then where would you be?

Harvard's Jennifer Pryor has put it this way:

> It can be very uplifting to rattle on about how we have to break through the glass ceiling to equal opportunity. But until you have had to dodge the shards of reality raining down on you as a result, you haven't confronted what your idealism costs. You may as well be shot up with Novocain before having sex. PITS was the crucial step in moving Alan beyond his idealistic misanthropy toward the realism and relevance of Franchisement.

It fell to historian Arthur Schlesinger, Jr., however, to draw the most suggestive comparison. Writing in the Spring 1998 issue of *Kennedyiana*, Schlesinger declared:

> The framers of our Constitution were not very sanguine about the citizenry unleashed by the fall of the English monarchy. Thus, it was that they drafted a Republican document of severe constraints on liberties and governance. Only with the Bill of Rights—the first ten amendments to the Constitution—did the Republic secure the freedoms that have become entrusted for safekeeping to the Kennedy family. In much the same way, Alan Gibb's initial drafting of the Franchisement charter betrayed what we might call a skeptical evaluation of mankind's capacity for

instinctive goodness and creativity. It was only when he amended his original vision with the PITS that he hazarded his trust in a fertile humanity.

And yet Gibb remained dissatisfied. He sensed a continuing blind spot in his vision. Acquaintances from the period describe him as "antsy," "annoying," and "really irritating." Linda McElligott, a Columbia colleague and author of *Omissive Language, Commissive Language—It's All Language*, relates he was so preoccupied with Franchisement's feared limitations that he couldn't even concentrate on having a casual drink with her. McElligott:

> Alan was an old-fashioned *caballero*. He took the curb side of the sidewalk when out with a woman, ran ahead to open doors, that kind of thing. Usually, anyway. But shortly after this PITS idea of his, he started acting distracted. If I asked him the time, he would just nod, as though it was sufficient to confirm both of us were still in that dimension. I'd tell him about some new relationship, and he would grunt as if it were one of my old ones. One night at this bar, we ordered two vodkas, the bartender gave me mine while he went to open a bottle for the other one, and Alan practically broke my fingers snatching the glass out of my hand. Then, a couple of weeks later in the same place, I went off to the Ladies Room and came back to find he'd drained my glass as well as his own. When I confronted him about it, he began arguing that I'd drunk it, that was why I had gone to pee in the first place. I have no doubt whatsoever that his odd behavior was caused by his feeling that he had to go even further than PITS if he wanted Franchisement to be something special.

Gibb himself has always declined comment about the two vodka incidents with McElligott, on one occasion calling her "a lush who could never get enough." But he has admitted to feeling "unsettled" during the period described.

> It was a confusing time. Sure, if I'd left it at the Personal Standings League and PITS, I could have made a few bucks. But

I wanted more than passing sensation, I wanted what so few of us have—enduring impact. That required a lot more than PITS, though. How do the kids say it? Bummer! Work and work and work. When was it ever going to end?

Fortunately for Franchisement customers, not with the PITS.

5

THE JOURNEY CONTINUES

NEW YORK METS   (Mascot: Fred Gibb Again)

Alan didn't know what to think when he saw his father again. On the one hand, it was an encounter he had been fantasizing about for years—through changing moods of joy, anger, and sullenness. On the other hand, his fantasies had been far less frequent with the passing of time, as though he had been reluctantly accepting Fred Gibb as an old suitcase consigned to a top closet shelf from where it might or might not ever be taken down again for use. On the third hand, there was his father's confusing appearance—that of a middle-aged man who had spent his time away gaining weight, pouches under his eyes, and a brand-new family.

Their meeting took place on the #7 train. Ever afterward Alan would entertain a suspicion (some flickering doubt from the corner of his eye) that Fred had spotted him first over the shoulders of the other standing passengers and had been on the verge of beating it down to the far end of the car when a sudden lurch by the train removed the people between them. Whether or not that was the case, Fred Gibb stood abruptly vulnerable next to a pole, two small boys and a freckled redheaded woman with bangs clustered around him. Alan felt none of the joy, anger, or sullenness he had practiced; instead, he blurted out an astonished "Hi!" that, initially at least, got more of a reaction from the redhead and the boys than from his father. The woman looked at him as if he were about to try to sell her something and the children frowned as though he were some subway specimen they had been warned to stay away from.

Finally, though, Fred snapped out of some wool gathering, stuck out his hand, and asked Alan how he had been doing. Before Alan could figure out an answer to that one, his father was introducing him to the woman named Casey and the kids named Richie and Gilbert. Awkwardness seemed to dissolve into deeper awkwardness. Alan didn't think a handshake really covered it with Fred after so much time, but he could hardly refuse to go along, either. He felt absolutely stupid bending down to accept the stiff mitts of the wary Richie and glum Gilbert, but what was he supposed to do—make ugly faces at them? And how was he supposed to react when Casey appraised him with a look harder than she had reserved for a yoyo peddler, nodded in confirmation of some bet she had apparently made with herself, and said: "You're the one who gets mustard all over his shirt!" Since Alan had never thought of himself in such terms, he stuttered that he was, unexpectedly secure in being someone for her he wasn't.

It turned out that Fred and his new family were on their way to the circus at Madison Square Garden, and Alan had to agree with the message between the lines that it wasn't the moment for him and his father to hash over old times, missing times, or new times. So he jotted down Fred's phone number (a Queens address) and promised to call the next day to set up a lunch. He didn't tell his mother about the encounter. He knew she didn't like him thinking about Fred, let alone running into him, and he wasn't in the mood for one of her lectures about building himself up for a letdown.

Alan called Fred the next day. Fred didn't sound enthusiastic, but they arranged to meet on the Brooklyn Promenade. He waited on the Promenade for a couple of hours—first telling himself the heavy rain was keeping Fred away, then that maybe he had gone to the wrong Promenade, then that maybe Richie and Gilbert had wanted to go to the circus again. None of the excuses he came up with made him less sad or less wet, and he was already sneezing by the time he returned home. Confined to bed with a heavy cold for a couple of days, he nevertheless resisted the impulse to call Fred's number again to demand an explanation for having been stood up. Instead, he found it more comfortable to accept Louise's first principle: If he *counted on* being let down from the start, he could feel only celebratory in the odd instance that somebody surprised him. Even Archie noticed that "something good" had happened to his stepson.

ATLANTA BRAVES   (Mascot: Connie Theodore)

Alan turned into a Lothario at college. Freed of Gloria Tavarez's exasperating daily presence and totally reconciled to the joys of losing (as opposed to her drab resignation to such a fate), he radiated a musk aroma of liberation. Going all the way was no longer a goal or even a challenge, it was an assumption. Where and with whom might not have been altogether immaterial, but they were in constant ferment, here there and everywhere, and he found himself more devoted to the movement for itself than to any of its particular stop-offs.

Then he met Connie Theodore, a sociology major not at all impressed by his campus reputation. Long and dark with a naturally puffy jaw and glowing brown eyes, Connie's first words to him when he asked if he could share her cafeteria table were: "If you know what you're going to do with your life." The fact was, Alan hadn't had a clue at that point, nor did he consider it vital to know until he was pushed off the campus in his cap and gown. His bafflement did nothing to charm Connie, who returned to underlining sentences in her textbook while he emptied his tray of his milk and tuna salad sandwich and took possession of his part of the table. When he observed that she demanded a high toll for sharing something that wasn't even legally hers, she sighed without looking up that "the air is for everybody, too, but if you don't control your part of it by contributing something new to it, you're just adding to the pollution."

Alan didn't know what to say, so he concentrated on unwrapping his sandwich. What he did know was that he was in love. Count the ways. She had the longest ink-smudged fingers he had ever seen. There was a merriment in her eyes that seemed to be an exquisite prize at the bottom of a pool for anyone daring enough to go that deep. She hardly knew him well enough to presume he was a loser, but she hadn't boxed herself out of that conclusion, either. And most important of all, she had insinuated he had to be somebody original to be worth her time or the time of anybody else on the planet.

Alan set out to be original. If he had to concede a certain crassness about his motives at first (to bed down Connie Theodore), he couldn't deny after a while that there was also something to be said for being more than just another luggage salesman, car salesman, school custodian, or any of the million and one variations on these trades to be found on Main Street, Wall Street, and Madison Avenue. But that was the easy part. It was the hard part that cemented his relationship with Connie—soliciting her ideas for what he might become. She was flattered to be asked, and without being coy about it, and began delving into the possibilities with him in the cafeteria, at an off-campus coffee shop, and in a couple of pubs. What he was good at, what he liked doing, what he had always harbored a secret desire to do—none of these starting points took them any appreciable distance. But rather than being discouraged, Connie Theodore grew more enthusiastic that he could so casually embody alienation, anomie, and other syndromes from her studies. Alan didn't mind her professional approach, undergraduate as it might have been; on the contrary, he couldn't remember anyone having defined him so romantically before. Even to himself he seemed seductively complicated, altogether phenomenal in some fundamentally dysfunctional way.

Finally came the morning in bed with Connie when, with the help of the *Wall Street Journal*, Alan knew what he wanted to do with his life. "What do you mean, you want to control the air?" she asked skeptically. Okay, he didn't mean the air literally, all that oxygen and breathing thing, what he had thought she was referring to that first day in the cafeteria. But weren't the psychologies of people a kind of invisible, unexplored space, too? By becoming a psychologist, he would be creating something out of nothing, and making a good living besides. He would be helping to shape the mental vagueness of individuals, laying a connective claim to their confusion and emptiness, and collecting some coin for his efforts.

It was a fateful decision. Connie turned her bare back on him and quickly disabused him of the notion that it was an invitation. It took some time, but Alan got over the rejection. In the end, he persuaded himself, she was mostly annoyed that he was more interested in the dynamics of disparate individuals than in the pushes and pulls of the established social networks she was studying. He was surprised Connie Theodore turned out to be so academically conventional.

CLEVELAND INDIANS   (Mascot: Theodore Herzl)

Although he soldiered on in graduate school, Alan had regular reminders that not everybody regarded him as an ideal psychologist. As Louise saw it, "you can't even pick up your socks after you, but you're going to pick up what people are thinking?" Archie's strongest endorsement was "try it, you don't like it, turn it in and try something else." As for his teachers, most of them sorted themselves out under the heading of I-Guess-He's-Okay-So-Pass-Him-On-And-We'll-Be-Okay. Making him most uncomfortable of all was Theodore Herzl.

Herzl was a gaunt Hasid with a bad case of acne who approached Alan prior to their first class together in The Psychology of Psychology. With an intemperance Alan came to intuit as a shield for the man's basic timidity with strangers, Herzl summarily informed him that his sole interest in psychology was to pick up a few negotiating moves for the day he took over his father's West 47th Street diamond business. "They come up to my father, they cry, they pull at their clothes, they pull their hair out," he explained as though asked something. "And of course he ends up giving them 10 percent over the 10 percent they've already extorted from the supplier. Middlemen, they call themselves. The only thing they're in the middle of is their fraud. Let them try that with me. They want to cry, I'll have a Kleenex for them. They want to pull out their hair, here, here's a pair of scissors. My father don't want to hear it. His ears have been closed since Moses came down from the mountain. But you got to use psychology with these crooks."

At first, Alan tried to ignore Herzl's regular jabs about why a *shnook* like him would be interested in, let alone grasp, psychological principles; he was too entranced by his new friend. Was it mere coincidence the Hasid had the same first name as Connie's last one? He didn't think so; that kind of continuity seemed pregnant with significance. And what about Herzl's own name—that of the pioneer of the Zionist state? Wasn't that a sign he was on the right track to do something original? And not least, here was someone who had embarked upon the graduate study program with the same sense of realism he had—psychology not as some abstract net for catching abstract butterflies, but psychology as a bug spray for bringing down moths and collecting a bounty on them.

Alan would have loved Herzl to open up on these and other subjects, but Herzl was not easy with his confidences. Regarding Connie Theodore's name, he said he didn't like talking about women to whom he wasn't married. He was named after the founder of Zionism? So who should he have been named after, the founder of Shinto? It was such a big thing to adapt psychology to business? Yeah, like using legs to walk. What Herzl preferred talking about was his disgust that somebody like Alan Gibb could be taking up desk space in the same classroom he was and that this was supposed to have given them something in common. "You talk to me because I'm safe," as he spat once. "Classes end, I go home to Crown Heights, you go home to your penthouse thinking of me sitting in my hovel reading the Torah and slopping down kosher mush. I'm a safe stereotype in your handicap of a life. You're fit for psychology like I am to hunt buffalo."

With enough repetition the tongue lashings eroded Alan's fascination with Herzl. The man wanted to be a caricature of a Jew? He wanted to wear his payehs, yarmulke, shiny coat, and the rest of his black uniform every day of his life? Fine. But don't blame

Alan Gibb if the caricature gained even more casual credibility. At least on a personal level, he began to avoid Herzl before and after classes. But his new distance also brought a solution to his Master's thesis—an in-depth analysis of the personality that found comfort in stereotypes. Entitled "The Mechanics of Caricatural Appeasement," the paper careened to the hypothesis that many individuals fulfilled aspirations to self-abuse by seeking to live up to society's basest depictions of them. As cases in point, Alan cited Theodore Herzl and a couple of other people he had heard about.

"The Mechanics of Caricatural Appeasement" barely did the job for Alan's degree. While the faculty review board found most of the paper's argumentation flimsy and whimsical, it also noted that Alan had shied away from projecting his conclusions into a broader social finding, thereby ratifying the unique role of the Psychology Department on campus and implicitly denying greater legitimacy for the Sociology Department. In explaining the C-Plus grade that gave Alan admission to the world of counseling, teaching, and promotional campaigns, board member Clarence Peizer said: "'The Mechanics of Caricatural Appeasement' makes a persuasively lukewarm case that you don't have to turn society upside down to get at a few disturbed individuals who just don't get it when they're being mocked, ridiculed, and insulted. As Gibb points out in relevant solipsistic language, their problem remains our problem and we should remain sensitive to their pain, however hard they don't feel it."

As happy as Alan was to have negotiated the obstacle of his thesis, he was almost as satisfied by Theodore Herzl's reaction to the paper. A few days after sending a copy to the man's Crown Heights home, he received his own envelope back with a Post Office stamp of RETURN TO SENDER. Mildly disappointed, he was about to dump the envelope in the garbage when he noticed extra lick marks around the flap. He slit open the envelope and found "The Mechanics of Caricatural Appeasement" torn into a dozen pieces. He was amazed the Post Office didn't have stronger regulations about people opening mail and then sending it back on the same stamp. He could understand why they were always grumbling about not having enough money.

CINCINNATI REDS   (Mascot: Lenore Kindall)

With his degree in hand, Alan decided it was time to strike out on his own. Louise wasn't happy to see him move out of the apartment, but Archie helped convince her that every young man needed to taste the rental experience. Alan's first choice for independent housekeeping was a furnished room on West 84th Street in Manhattan (a mere eight blocks away from his Franchisement vision years later). He didn't delude himself that the place had any personality, which was just as well since the best it did in that category was to provide a scampering cockroach herd every time he returned home after sunset and turned on a light. The important thing, he reminded himself, was the personality *he* projected over the claustrophobic cluster of a daybed, two beach chairs, a faded print of a schooner, a cankered sideboard, chipped kitchen table, and frayed linoleum.

The future Father of Franchisement was able to afford the room thanks to his first graduate position—as a copywriter for the city agency charged with popularizing municipal logos and emblems. Assigned to the Fire Department account, he researched the historical precedents for painting engines red, for keeping ladders horizontal rather than diagonal while transporting them through traffic, and for installing poles in firehouses. Misgivings that such trivia hardly required a sheepskin-bearing psychologist ran up against Pete Anderson, the office manager. A craggy-faced man with twinkling blue eyes and a voice hoarse from 30 years of Lucky Strikes, Anderson reminded Alan that "citizens are psyches with votes, the way to direct those votes is to calm the psyches, and the way to calm them is to tell them why we do things the way we do them." When Alan admitted bafflement at this explanation, Anderson turned a frightening crimson for a moment, counted loudly to three, took a deep breath, and tried again. "What do you think would happen, Gibb, if the Fire Department put black engines on the street tomorrow? You'd get mass panic, that's what. Our citizenry would think of the Fire Department in terms of charred bodies, hearses, and death. If it was pink instead of black, they'd say the Department was THAT WAY, know what I mean? But when you stick to red and explain the status quo to the citizenry, it sleeps better at night. And as the person doing the explaining, you're contributing to its mental health."

Alan rarely came away from his pep talks with Anderson more enlightened than when he had entered the man's office. But he clung to the consolation that as long as he was researching material with potential interest to human beings, he was staying within a psychological orbit. In his first few weeks at the agency he also had the distraction of Lenore Kindall, responsible for the Parks Department account. A tiny brunette with a mole in the configuration of Chad on her left shoulder, Lenore immediately embraced him as a special orientation project, seeing him through the dos and don'ts of account research techniques, approaches to fellow employees, and telephone etiquette. Would her helpfulness and constant flirting have been incentive enough for Alan to make her his first guest in his furnished room? Undoubtedly. But he was also titillated by how much of a raving paranoid Lenore Kindall was. Seldom did she impart a word to him without first swiveling completely around to make sure nobody else was listening. In drilling him in the intricacies of the intercom system, she was incapable of lifting the receiver without listening for the telltale click of a wiretap. He was little better off asking her a question. No matter how innocuous the query, she seemed to lick every side of it with her tongue, responding only after she had satisfied herself it was completely flavorless.

Thus, when Alan invited Lenore to his room, he had more than one agenda. Yes, he wanted to see her live up to her promise to "do wonders" with some canned ravioli, and yes, he wanted to roll around on the daybed with her. But after so many humdrum days at the agency, he also wanted to practice what graduate school had supposedly prepared him to do—study a human personality up close, hypothesize where its rotten core might lead its carrier, and jot down notes about his findings. To his surprise, Lenore didn't mind; in fact, once he told her what he planned after they had eaten and fucked, she sighed in relief that they would be getting what she called his "itch" out of the way on their first date. Other guys had been depressingly evasive on that score, she informed him, pretending to ignore her periodic checks at front door peepholes or her terror when some token clerk or movie house cashier eyed her too steadily. With what outcome? They had saved up all their reservations about her until their third or fourth date, and then suddenly they had claimed to be seeing her for the first time as they hurried off for a cab. At least with him, she told Alan as she emptied two cans of ravioli into a full pot of boiling water, there could be no ambiguity about his suspicions that her elevator didn't rise all the way to the top floor.

Before such an open invitation Alan took his own direct tack: *Did* she admit she might have some issues in the paranoia department? Lenore's smile was pitying. Maybe she shouldn't have been so patronizing because Alan was so young and inexperienced, she said, but she also couldn't help feeling Americans at any age should have been ready to ferret out the perils around them. What perils, he asked cautiously. Name them, she shrugged. Who *wasn't* out to get agency employees? There was no need to think in terms of vast international Communist conspiracies in Moscow. Enemies were far closer at hand. What about the newsstand dealer who kept a record of the papers she bought every morning? What about her corner grocer who only the day before had failed her test when she had asked simply for "beer" and he had gone immediately to the brand she had bought the previous trip? And the people at the office—why were they so interested in what she was working on for the Parks Department? Just because they wanted to know more about the statue of Balto in Central Park? When people told you they wanted to know more about old, dead, bronzed dogs, you could be pretty sure they were the wrong kind of fleas.

Alan was grateful for Lenore's sincerity, and it almost carried him through her version of ravioli. But he was also troubled by his own place in her dark universe: What made him different to her? "There's something traditional about you," she said, leaning over the table to kiss him and pat his clenched fists. "You believe in what people always believed in."

When she put her foot between his legs under the table, Alan held back from asking what that belief was.

6

LOCATION, LOCATION, LOCATION,

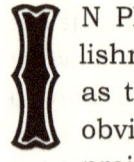N PERSON, DR. Alan Gibb looks too slight for his accomplishments. In the face of the historical record establishing him as the only issue of Fred and Louise Gibb, and despite the obvious hundreds of dollars spent on his cowboy shirt, he projects the air of a younger brother wearing hand-me-downs. He never seems too far from apologizing for the attention showered on him, or from simply wondering why people are around him at all. When his wife Connie interrupts to serve tea, he watches her from his leather chair in puzzlement that she has shared so much of his time on earth, perhaps never to know for sure which one of them might have chosen more sagely. The vanity and the humility have become too intertwined for facile reading.

As soon as Connie leaves the room again, he unwraps a red Jolly Rancher. "I like these red ones," he says. "But even they're nothing compared to the old Charms. Remember Charms? I miss Charms."

In the days shortly after coming up with his Positional Identity Trait Signs (PITS), as Linda McElligott and others have attested, he was missing much more than Charms. He was only too aware that if he didn't go further than PITS, he would have been Moses settling for seven commandments, Columbus dropping anchor at Malta, and Alexander Graham Bell patenting a megaphone. He didn't need McElligott or anybody else to tell him he was at a critical crossroads: his body was revolting in anxiety, making him less than an ideal companion for social functions. When alone, he drifted through hours in his furnished room throwing darts or seeking out revival houses for old movies where the protagonist, having endured humiliations of all stripes, was finally able to turn fervid eyes to the camera and exclaim: "I've got it!"

Except that Alan Gibb didn't get it. Edward G. Robinson as Doctor Ehrlich, Greer Garson as Marie Curie, Montgomery Clift as Sigmund Freud all proved useless as inspirations. They got it, he reminded himself, because they had known what they were going to get as soon as they looked at their scripts. His script for Franchisement, on the other hand, wasn't complete yet. He was far from even contemplating what actor might eventually play him on the screen.

It was the president of the Ecumenical Council on Mental Observances, Father Benjamin Acocella, S.J., who helped Gibb define more precisely what remained missing from his Franchisement vision. Acocella:

> Alan had been hinting for weeks that he'd come up with
> something that, he said, would "make dogmeat" out of other
> traditional observances. His passion disturbed me. Whenever
> I saw him on the Columbia campus, he all but smashed an
> elbow into my ribs daring me to guess what he was stewing. If
> I'm grateful for anything today, it's that I didn't react to these
> provocations and belt him in the mouth. If I had, the world might
> have come to Franchisement much later than it did.

Deciding that Acocella could be trusted with his secret, Gibb invited him one evening for a stroll in Central Park. Although confessing to "some uneasiness" about the invitation, Acocella sensed it would be the best way of getting to the roots of his associate's recently odd behavior.

> As we walked along, Alan began outlining his theory of Franchisement. I was flabbergasted. I heard Ignatius. I heard the Cabbala. I heard Zoroastrianism. I heard a peyote incantation. I heard so many things. What took longer for me to hear was the despair between the lines of his triumphalism. He had worked out everything, but felt as though he had worked out nothing. For him Franchisement—at that moment in time—had turned into an immaculately produced and upholstered vehicle that he didn't dare start in the showroom for fear that he'd never get through the front door.

Acocella was more than familiar with Gibb's apprehensions. It had been less than a year since he had wrestled with a similar problem on the issue of admitting Scientology into his ecumenical council.

> That one was a toughie. On the one hand, it was a claptrap hustle that relied on lawsuits and white Van Heusen shirts for sustenance. Something was definitely missing in the free will and spiritual departments. On the other hand, we had received tons of affidavits from movie stars and their dieticians attesting to a belief in warrior extraterrestrials who served as a kind of guardian angel force. But where we were stymied was that we couldn't find an explicit connection between these warriors and the posh villas where the movie stars and the dieticians lived. And until we could make that link, we couldn't in good conscience let them join the council. I discerned the same absence of a connection in Franchisement. Alan had met the first two requirements of a visionary system by coming up with a mythology and a theology, but the ritual—the actual physiological means of participation by customers—simply wasn't there. I told him right off the bat that without the ritual, he didn't have a prayer in Hell or Lethe or Non-Being that the public would buy any of his wares.

So how was that obstacle overcome?

We'd been walking in the park a long time. I was so mesmerized
by what he was saying it took me a while to realize we had gotten
lost. I heard no traffic sounds from Fifth Avenue or Central
Park West, couldn't see the usual buildings over the trees for
navigating. And to make things worse, there was these slugs who
had been following us for a good 15 or 20 minutes, about five of
them. They didn't look like the kind who wanted to know when
we'd be holding our next council seminar.

Gibb recorded the same pregnant moment in *You're a Peewee,
I'm a Bambino.*

The priest wasn't listening to me anymore. So much for that
caring shepherd, I thought. All he kept muttering was, "I think
we're lost, Al- an." Lost! We're in Central Park, for Jesus Christ
sake! A rube just off the bus from Los Alamos knows where he'd
be if he was walking in Central Park! But then, as he started
going on about this gang of nitwits behind us, I played back what
he had said. If you're lost, it occurred to me, you don't know your
location. And there it was! Thanks to a lot of old lady fretting
from Acocella, I came up with my missing link—the principle of
LOCATION!

Gibb had to spend almost three hours at the local precinct going
over the stickup that had left him without a wallet and Acocella
with a fractured skull. He couldn't wait to get back to his furnished
room on Amsterdam Avenue to spool out the implications of his
epiphany in the park. As he recalled reminding his walls:

Since Neanderthal days, the primary human impulse has
been to locate. Modern beings endeavor to locate in the best
neighborhood, try to locate a good job, want to locate the G-spot.
Underline that: *They* want to do the locating. No charlatan
coming along to say *they are located* in Taurus or Scorpio, like

they had nothing to do with it except take a walk around under the constellations. What modern human beings want is a say in their own pigeon-holing.

In short, the principle of Location enabled Franchisement customers to make the ultimate connection of being ACTIVE adepts. "They didn't have to just lie there anymore," as Harvard's Jennifer Pryor has pointed out. "They could express their own volatile needs without having to clear it first with some preemptive Need Keeper." For Benjamin Acocella, who ironically didn't know how critical he had been to define the concept until he came off the critical list, Location was "the ritual—the dance between celebrant and parishioner, the chicken's blood between Baron Samedi and spaced out moaners, the sacrificial knife between the Aztec shaman and the virgin stretched out on a stone slab. It made Franchisement inter-connective."

One practical problem remained. Gibb had already made his vision both SIMPLE and COMPLICATED. Wouldn't Location threaten that fine balance? What appeal to customers could possibly embrace both the simple and the complicated, yet build on them? Indicative of his mood in the wake of the park mugging, Gibb didn't permit such quandaries to depress him; quite the contrary, he relished the challenge. "Once I came to grip with the fact that Franchisement couldn't just be me, that my customers had to be a pro-active part of the process," as he wrote in *You're a Peewee, I'm a Bambino*, "I had to open myself to letting them spark my final epiphany."

And spark it they did. Their names are as lost to history as that of the boy at the Broadway and West 76th Street bus stop, but from what Gibb has admitted, they were two seniors in Columbia sweatshirts who happened to be checking out their Ontology 414 grades as he was walking down the hall of the Philosophy building. The sudden whoop that exploded from the pair froze Gibb in his loafers and white socks. They had both passed. They were JOYOUS. They were FREE.

And like that, the last piece of the Franchisement monument settled into its foundation.

Other systems, it struck Gibb, were not merely dictatorial in imposing precepts and interpretations of the precepts; they also proposed readings that could be SAD, PAINFUL, or just plain BAD. Who wanted that kind of evaluation, even if the customer did have something of an active role in eliciting it? Where Franchisement had to differ in its proactive and personal dynamics, it was suddenly clear, was in ensuring that customers would always be FREE to seek the reading that would render them JOYOUS. There had to be completely POSITIVE energies from the beginning, not only because a credit card number checked out, but also because there were definitely going to be POSITIVE energies at the end of a consultation, as well. Mental rose petals had to litter the entire course.

Indiana's Sidney Willinger recalled his experiences in this connection in *When Winning Teams Are the Only Teams—Franchisement in Mass Culture:*

I didn't tell Alan I had an academic interest in his research.
My Leisure Activities faculty had grown the slightest bit stale,
I thought, from the usual family and mass media things, and
I was looking to plug into some new circuit of human play.
Without giving away too much about me, I'll just say I selected a
characterology from the Personal Standings League and provided
enough clues that Alan was able to recommend a PITS for me.
But the PITS he chose cast such an unfavorable light on my
Personal Standings League selection that I came off sounding like
a creep who hung around schoolyards. As soon as he sensed my
discomfort, Alan told me to go to another team. We did that four
times before I was satisfied, and not once did he insinuate that I
was being difficult. As he kept saying, it was up to me to LOCATE
where I wanted to be, nobody could do it for me, not even him.

Wall Street analyst Jack Fenaughty has seen the process in a much simpler light. Fenaughty:

Behind every great stock there's the nurturing attitude that the
customer is always right. By letting these people keep choosing

their Personal Standings League team until they come across one
that doesn't say lousy things about them, Gibb is just adhering
to sound business principle. At the same time, of course, he's
also establishing that spirit of mutual supportiveness that will
guarantee the customer will come running back when he's not
feeling so goddamn joyous and free.

7

THE JOURNEY CONTINUES FURTHER

ST. LOUIS CARDINALS   (Mascot: Matthew Pine)

Alan left his city agency job after four months. For one thing, he lost his ability to rationalize his research projects on pikes, hoses, and hydrants as beneficial to the career of a psychologist. For another thing, he was fired. By his own reckoning, he could have survived Lenore Kindall's denouncing him as an industrial spy working for the city of Cincinnati: Lenore had leveled similar accusations at everyone in the office at one time or another, to little lasting damage beyond several investigations and one suicide. But already dispirited by the triviality of his daily tasks, he had felt no obligation to be as philosophical about her smears as his co-workers had become. As he told Lenore one morning while the two of them were waiting for an elevator, there was a fine line between her pathology and the legally libelous, and she had crossed it. When Lenore entered the elevator car with another of her pitying laughs for him, Alan made the decision to cross his own line—charging into the office of Pete Anderson and accusing the manager of turning a blind eye to a clinical case on the premises that required immediate treatment. Once the blood had returned to his veins, Anderson made three points. One, Lenore Kindall was as mentally balanced as anybody in the agency. Two, anybody could purchase a university degree claiming he was a psychologist, but it was the psychologies themselves, including the aberrant ones, that kept any metropolis going. And three, since Alan had clearly been uncomfortable since joining the agency at having to shelve his elitism and commit himself to the needs of the citizenry, it was just as well he go elsewhere to mine his talents.

He ended up mining them in a brewery under the Williamsburg Bridge. As the ad in the New York *Post* put it: "WANTED IMMEDIATELY—PSYCHOLOGIST WITHOUT HEAVY SALARY DEMANDS FOR EXCITING NEW PROJECT IN CONSUMER TESTING." Alan and the brewery's personnel director, Matthew Pine, hit it off at once. A linebacker gone to seed, most conspicuously in the gut, Pine could hardly wait for Alan to finish recounting his academic career, his previous employment at the city agency, and his belief that the business of psychology and the psychology of business would always be different sides of the same coin. The man finally jumped up from his desk with relief when Alan mentioned a salary figure that turned out to be only $10,000 more than the brewery intended paying. "You're coming awfully close to saying the right thing, Professor Gibb," Pine drawled in a rich baritone. "Lower your sights a little and we might just torpedo that cruiser right out of the water. What do you say?"

Alan never quite recalled what he did say, although it was evidently an encouragement for Pine to conclude he had accepted the $10,000 lower salary and to move on to a description of the task at hand. Then and there he was enchanted by the title "Professor"— the first time anybody had ever assumed that was what he was. As for the job that needed doing at the brewery, Pine explained that the company had been coming under vicious attacks for sweetening its products with chemicals that, according to the usual crackpots, accelerated inebriation. It was the brewery's contention that the problem rested with beer as such—that it had taken on such a glamorous mystique in the average American household that consumers were already emotionally tipsy before they cracked open their first can, making the subsequent digestion of the sweeteners irrelevant, immaterial, and grossly hypothetical. What the company needed from Professor Gibb was a controlled demonstration that would shut up the honkers and restore some corporate luster.

Alan didn't come up with a solution overnight. In fact, over his first couple of weeks testing company products, what he mainly came up with was a series of headaches. But given the fervid guarantees of Pine and other brewery executives, he attributed them more to his lack of familiarity with the company brands than to any dangerous level of chemical additives. Finally, he devised his test. With the help of a company lie detector called a mendachrometer, he proposed seating a number of guinea pigs before mugs containing beers from four different companies and, through variations on what brands the subjects were told they were drinking, establish objectively that his employer's added chemicals were far subordinate in their effect to a general euphoria over the prospect of just being able to down a few brews.

The short of it was that the test was a tremendous success. With company camera crews filming every sip, all the demonstration subjects were shown to be well on their way to intoxication before they even reached for their tankards. When the results were included in a nationally televised commercial, with Alan standing gravely in the background in a white smock and holding a clipboard, the attacks on the brewery subsided. The company was so elated with the response that it came up with a new slogan—WE'RE NOT RESPONSIBLE, YOU ARE.

Because he had hired Alan, Matthew Pine was promoted to Vice-President for Popular Entertainment. Pine in turn recommended that Alan be given a $2,500 bonus for his good work. Alan was disappointed that the company board approved only $350 and a free tape of the commercial, but he regarded it as a professional advancement when Pine assured him he could have a free-lance title of Consultant to the brewery and would be the first psychologist contacted if there was ever again need to counter some scurrilous propaganda campaign. As he put it at their last meeting: "Standing down doesn't mean standing idle, Professor. Let them try to strafe us again and we'll fill the skies with more lethal birds than they see in their nightmares." Alan said he looked forward to that day.

CHICAGO CUBS   (Mascot: Casey Williams)

For weeks after being let go by the brewery, Alan felt on the verge of professional vindication. If his money was still low and he had no immediate job prospects, he was able to confirm what he was capable of every time he passed a TV set in an appliance store window and saw the commercial with his test. His self-confidence ballooned even more when somebody from his building or from the Unemployment Office eyed him with the suspicion of having seen him somewhere. Then Casey Williams called.

Alan did not recognize the name. He was too busy being grateful that Matthew Pine had recommended him to somebody. He also considered it a small marvel that Casey Williams had put up with an old goat named Belluno on the pay phone in the hall to get through to him. The icing on the cake was the Park Avenue skyscraper where he went for his appointment with her. Walking through the revolving doors and announcing his destination to a lobby receptionist, he had never felt so close to real power—or to his potential use of it. He thought it a happy omen that Williams should be working for an outfit called Miracle Merchandising, Inc.

Then the revelations came. The Casey Williams who greeted him at the elevator bank on the 69th floor with a stevedore's handshake was the freckled redhead he had last seen standing next to his father and her sons Richie and Gilbert on the #7 train. With a quizzical smile at his reaction she told him without preamble that she still had Richie and Gilbert but not Fred Gibb; the last she had heard of his father, she said as she conducted him down a carpeted hall to her office, he had been working for some hippie knapsack company in New Jersey. Did Alan still spill mustard over his shirt?

Alan didn't have time to say. Once directed to a deep leather chair in front of the desk nameplate CASSANDRA WILLIAMS,

BALLBREAKER-IN-CHIEF, his priority was to listen. How had his name come up between her and Matthew Pine? Matthew was her big brother at an AA chapter and had been helping her stay off booze for years. Why had his name come up with Matthew Pine? Because Miracle Merchandising, Inc. needed a one-shot promotional campaign that would be solidly grounded in all the psychological verities, and Pine had mentioned him as effective and cheap. What was the nature of the campaign? To restore miracles to popular culture.

When Alan confessed he hadn't been thinking much lately about miracles, Casey said that was all right, that his oversight was symptomatic of the problem requiring corrective measures. What she wanted to do, she explained, was to "market a mood—the idea that anything is possible because this is the United States of America and the United States of America has much bigger fish to fry than just opportunity." What bigger fish might she be thinking of? She shrugged as though it should have already occurred to him: "The right to pursue miracles on a daily basis."

Impressed as he was by such an ambition, Alan had to wonder how a greater openness to miracles in the national psyche could benefit Miracle Merchandising, Inc. When Casey's reply was a languid wave toward a display case against the wall, he stood up for a closer inspection. What he saw were shelves crammed with every conceivable kind of knick-knack: a wizard's hat, a thimble of water labeled as having been parted from the Red Sea, figurines representing Jesus Christ and Lazarus, a miniature alchemy set, differently colored statues of Our Lady of Guadalupe, Our Lady of Lourdes, and Our Lady of Fatima. "The market's dried up for that crap," Casey informed him. "The only miracle left in them is we still sell a few of them every month." But more than that, she added, even if her buyers were still moving such curios, they remained physical objects, and she was bent on having the company make a qualitative leap to psychological product, to the "miracle mood" she had mentioned. "No manufacturing or warehouse maintenance costs, no shipping charges—the overhead savings alone will make them forget the loaves and the fishes!"

When Alan professed a second doubt about a belief in miracles reflecting any of the psychological standards he had been schooled in, Casey gave him the same condescending smile she had bestowed on him in the #7 train and asked whether he wanted to make a few grand. Once she received the answer she wanted, she got down to the nitty-gritty: His job was to come up with any concept at all that seemed unlikely to the point of impossibility and that the whole nation could root for being achieved. The company would then plot a campaign around his choice and reap profits from advertisers seeking to be official sponsors of the feat.

Alan felt optimistic leaving Casey's office that first day, but the assignment proved daunting. For weeks, she rejected every one of his proposals out of hand, and not always with grace. For Casey Williams, there was nothing at all miraculous about someday landing on the moon; hundreds of millions of governments dollars and technological advances made that inevitable. There was nothing miraculous, either, about the United States one day being able to get out of Vietnam; the Vietcong, North Vietnamese army, and fragging epidemic within the U.S. armed forces made that only logical. And don't tell her about the Nixon administration maybe convening a love-in with anti-war demonstrators: She herself had accepted Gilbert's poncho, sandals, and long hair around the house, and she could testify from personal experience that it was more resignation than miracle. What was the matter with him? Wasn't there anybody on the Gibb family tree capable of sprouting in the spring?

Then Alan hit upon the psychological commodity he had been seeking. Suppose, he suggested, the company got behind an atrocious baseball team and promoted it as the year's World Series winner? Wouldn't the sheer popularity of the sport relieve Miracle Merchandising, Inc. of the need to justify or explain its choice? Not every American believed in the Lady of Fatima or even knew in what region of Egypt she was supposed to have appeared, but even non-baseball fans had heard of Cooperstown. The company wouldn't have to spend a dime on explaining why waiting for a miracle was necessary.

Casey had one doubt right away: What team? Alan hoped he sounded as supercilious as he felt; she had it coming after all her condescension toward him. Who else but the team that had become synonymous with mediocrity and worse—the Chicago Cubs? Casey needed a moment of swinging back and forth in her desk chair to ponder the nomination. Alan could hear such omissive words as *ridiculous* and *asshole* dying in the air over the desk between them, and he knew why: He was shooting them down with his miracle ack-ack. Finally, Casey nodded. "This doesn't work, Gibb," she confided to him, "it'll be your balls. You won't even have a knapsack company in Jersey to run to."

Miracle Merchandising, Inc. began deluging the media with stirring tales about ailing children, shut-ins, and popular actors expressing faith in the Cubs. A San Diego doctor told a press conference he could think of only one reason why Jimmy Bledsoe, a 93-pound victim of leukemia, had survived an operation with a 95-percent fatality probability: The Cubs cap the boy had worn on the operating table. 78-year-old Carmen Singh testified in a Flushing courtroom that the assailants who had broken into her house would have bludgeoned her to death if one of them hadn't noticed that the baseball bat in his hand had been signed by Cubs star Ernie Banks. Charlton Heston, an Illinois native, confessed the Cubs had taught him everything he knew about acting. Casey became a frequent guest on the network morning shows, where she drummed home the message that if the Cubs could do it in the National League, America could do it in the world league, and any time it wanted. As for Alan, he wasn't sure about the cause and effect when the Cubs did indeed start winning consistently, holding first place through the summer months; what he did know was that the people in his building, even the crabby goat Belluno, were back to greeting him heartily whenever he passed them on the stoop or in the hallway. If he didn't achieve quite the visibility he had gained with the brewery commercials, he never stopped pointing out he had been the first on the Upper West Side to fill his window with the poster MIRACLES START WITH THE CUBS AND END WITH YOU. Belluno wasn't the only one who had to admit this probably made Alan the insider on the miracle campaign he claimed to be.

As it turned out, Belluno was also the one who knocked on his door the morning Casey called with bad news. A bewhiskered

70-year-old whose teeth ran to the same yellow his sleeveless undershirts did, Belluno couldn't resist a cackle in reporting that Alan was wanted on the hall phone by "someone who says she wants to break your balls." Alan didn't need Casey to tell him that the Mets had passed the Cubs into first place; he had already heard that from a radio blaring into his window from the stoop the night before. What he needed even less was Casey's threat that, unless Chicago regained the lead and for keeps, he would never work again in New York. Whatever the association in his mind (it could have been Belluno's yellow teeth as much as anything), Alan chose that moment on the hall phone to clarify an old misunderstanding with Casey. "I don't spill mustard on my shirt," he told her firmly. "I might've come close, but I never did it."

By the time the Mets had completed snatching the miracle away from the Cubs and had won the World Series, both Casey and Alan were busy on other projects. For Miracle Merchandising, Inc., the horse might have been wrong but the race had been right, and Casey's exposure on network television enabled her to form a partnership with the Third Pentecostal Church of Oklahoma City. The company soon became active throughout the southwest selling physical *and* psychological miracle commodities: bottled tears from the joy of spiritual rebirth for those of a practical turn of mind, commercials plugging imminent liberation through the Rapture for those of a more attitudinal bent. Meanwhile, Alan was turned down for one job after another, and so summarily he knew Casey had made good on her threats. His last doubt evaporated after even his file officer at the Unemployment Office asked if it was true—as an anonymous phone call had reported—that he had been promoting a miracle by the Cubs rather than the Mets. Months of languor followed. He became idle, penniless, and, finally, homeless. Although Louise tossed him a few dollars every so often from what she called her Special Benefits Fund and Archie assured him he could borrow any car in the GM showroom he wanted to make an impression on a prospective employer, he felt fated to be wandering down a road that ended with a men's shelter. Disputing his destiny, he told himself, would have only made it harder in the long run to make some money from his travails.

And in fact, it was one night on a dormitory cot in the city's Municipal Inn #3, while clutching his duffel bag to his chest, that Alan glowed with a genuine peace. Unlike his various earlier awarenesses about being a loser, this time he swelled up with the serenity of having accepted himself as part of a *tradition* of losing. Miracles simply weren't in his genes; he was Fred Gibb's son, and Fred Gibb had obviously had no better luck with Cassandra Williams than he had had. Meditating on this lineage brought him such an overwhelming sense of belonging that, as a brute of a rummy named Cleaver rousted the sleeper in the adjoining cot, he knew, when it came his turn, he would never surrender his duffel bag to Cleaver without a fight. His father might not have actually sold him the bag, but for all practical psychological purposes he had. And that was the only practicality that counted, wasn't it?

8

AT HOME
WITH
DR. ALAN GIBB

R. ALAN GIBB is feeling playful. By his own admission, he hasn't personally conducted a Franchisement session in years, leaving that to his employees in Duluth, Minnesota and Enid, Oklahoma while he has tended to administrative and expansion matters. But today he has arranged for a call to be rerouted to his Fifth Avenue apartment so he can, as he describes it, "feel the old feeling." When his wife Connie plugs in the console on the table next to him, he traces his hand in the air over all the buttons, searching for Conference Call the way he might play eeny-meeny-miney-mo with a tank of live lobsters in a fish restaurant. Finally, he finds the Conference Call button. The voice coming out of the machine has a heavy German accent.

CUSTOMER: *Franchisement Central?*

Gibb cannot help winking to those around him as he turns on the recorder and timer plugged into the phone. Seated on the couch, Connie is already amused by the spectacle about to unfold. There is no doubting that she has been a party to such follies before, and has come to consider them part of her husband's private charm.

GIBB: *More central than you know. What is your credit card number, please?*

The voice reads out numbers and the expiration date. Gibb tries to be soundless about opening another Jolly Rancher. Who is to say he hasn't already inferred key features of the caller's personality in the manner the numbers have been given? There is the slightest of liquid intakes as he drops the yellow Jolly Rancher onto his tongue. The customer finally stops talking.

GIBB: *And how can I help you today, sir?*

CUSTOMER: *I've always thought of myself as a New York Yankees Personality with a Hitting PITS.*

Gibb rolls his eyes. He will explain later that this is the most common self-identity among middle-age and older males and that most of the consultation with such customers is spent bringing them around to the admission that their unhappiness is caused by what he terms an "over-belief" in that image. Generally speaking, it is a syndrome not all that removed from the ancient belief of Minor League people that they were actually Major League people.

GIBB: *Well, that sounds like a good start to me.*

CUSTOMER: *Accent on the start. Where do I go from here?*

GIBB: *Well, where would you like to go?*

CUSTOMER: *Let me put it this way. There are too many dreamers in this world. The ones who don't think they can wish everything to be nice think they can bomb everything into being nice. I reject both courses as being dangerously unrealistic. Nothing is for free in the butcher shop. You have to give away the meat in the window if you want people to come in and buy what you have inside. You get a little sawdust on your shoes, that's called politics.*

GIBB: *That's an interesting viewpoint, sir. And frankly, not one I would associate with the Hitting PITS of a Yankees Personality.*

CUSTOMER: *Well, there you are! Something's wrong!*

Connie proffers a notebook to Gibb. He waves it off. He is having too much fun improvising from his years of stored knowledge.

GIBB: *Then suppose we try a Pitching PITS.*

CUSTOMER: *Yeah? What will that give me?*

GIBB: *The same realistic aggressiveness. But with the veneer of suggesting that other people in the world are as important as you are.*

CUSTOMER: *Okaay . . .*

GIBB: *In this way you can advocate the bombing of some annoying country . . . Name one.*

CUSTOMER: *Any one. Doesn't make a difference.*

GIBB: *Okay. You can advocate blowing some country to kingdom come, but make it sound like an altruistic act. It won't all come back on you and it won't make you sound like one of these cavemen dreamers you were mentioning before.*

CUSTOMER: *Yeah, but what about if I come off sounding too altruistic? Then they'll think I'm one of these left-wing dreamers.*

GIBB: *Keep your eye on the ball, sir. If you have bodies heaped on rubble at the end, who's going to remember how you got there? I've heard that every city in Europe . . . You're from Europe, I gather?*

CUSTOMER: *Why is that your business?*

GIBB: *Okay, it isn't. Sorry about that. But my point is that I've heard all these European cities have squares and things and that there are all kinds of little streets that bring you to them.*

CUSTOMER: *Yeah?*

GIBB: *Well, you're just taking a little street nobody else has. What's important is that you end up in the fountain in the square.*

There is a silence from the other end. Gibb suddenly shows intensity as he stares at the Conference Call button. For all the playfulness behind the idea of speaking to the customer personally, he remains a proud man persuaded of his vision and will not easily suffer rejection. Connie, on the other hand, seems less apprehensive. She has found a liver spot or some other growth on the back of her hand that has distracted her. She turns her hand to the window light for a better look. She doesn't like what she sees.

CUSTOMER: *I see your point.*

Gibb is so relieved he does something he rarely does—he crunches his yellow Jolly Rancher with his back teeth. He will acknowledge later that it has been months since he hadn't sucked one completely through to the end. (Somewhat more defensively, he will attribute the change to "that lemon flavor—it seems to go on forever sometimes.")

GIBB: *Then you will let yourself feel the joy you've earned?*

CUSTOMER: *Location, right?*

GIBB: *That's our objective, sir.*

CUSTOMER: *A Yankee with a Pitching PITS! I hadn't thought of it. We can blow the buggers off the face of the earth and not feel like we're kidding ourselves.* Realpolitik!

GIBB: *Does that make you feel free?*

CUSTOMER: *Oh, Christ, yes! Thanks a lot!*

There is the funneled sound of the phone being hung up. Gibb doesn't move for a long moment. Then he points to the credit card timer that is still ticking. He looks gleeful to be gaining the extra seconds of profit after the break in the connection. Connie doesn't share his satisfaction. She is still looking at the back of her hand against the reflection from the window. But it is not the spot or whatever that still preoccupies her. Now she seems simply baffled that she never before saw the back of her hand in such a light.

9

THE JOURNEY CONTINUES FURTHER STILL

HOUSTON ASTROS   (Mascot: Ray Heinz)

Alan Gibb's diagonal journey from Municipal Inn #3 on the Lower East Side to Columbia University on the Upper West Side of Manhattan began when he talked night supervisor Reggie Wynn into letting him help around the shelter. To Wynn's response that he was better off out in the street, Alan insisted he preferred being indoors, that, thieves and junkies notwithstanding, the darkest of building vestibules and roomiest of cardboard boxes didn't afford the shelter's temperature-controlled comforts. What he didn't tell the skeptical Wynn was that he also wanted to stick around Municipal Inn #3 for the access it provided to its nightly inmates. As he had reminded himself the night he was defending his duffel bag against the brute named Cleaver, he was a trained worker of the human psyche, and it was time for him to get back to what he knew best—his career. What better living laboratory than the 80 winos, psychos, and schizoids who trooped through the big green doors under police guard every 7:00 P.M.?

Assisting Wynn brought the results Alan had hoped, if not exactly in the way he had foreseen. He was unpleasantly surprised, for instance, to discover that "assisting" meant answering all the bathroom calls, patrolling the two dormitories with his flashlight every hour on the hour, and doubling as the house exterminator whenever somebody complained the floor was moving more than it should have. As for Wynn, he was generally content to record the names of the overnights delivered by the police vans, confirm their number equaled that of the available cots, lock up the metal screen dividers, then retire to his Four Roses and portable TV until dawn. His rule of thumb (as he passed it on to Alan, more in the spirit of assuring enforcement than of imparting pure knowledge) was to give the shouters three strikes. If they didn't cry out a fourth time, it could be assumed they had handled the molester or DTs on their own. Alan thought that outlook a little lazy, but kept his mouth shut.

To his consternation, so did everybody else. Although he had anticipated some reluctance on the part of the overnights to discuss the psychological debacles that had led them to the shelter, Alan had been optimistic that with the right word here and a fortuitous gesture there he would be able to break through decades of addictions and derangements to chart one or two specific personality arcs. But even the overnights who didn't snarl at him, threaten him, or try to hit him up for a few bucks mostly just gaped at him, their rheumy eyes as seeing as those of a cod on ice. Whatever topic he brought up to establish a conversational bond—sports, the crisis in the Middle East, doing the commercials for the Brooklyn brewery—the reaction was seldom more than the click of a bad dental plate.

Then one night, a former judge turned alcoholic, Ray Heinz, leveled the stare of stares. Sitting on the cot closest to the metal screen divider, Heinz fended off every invitation to examine his insufficiencies with the most soundlessly emphatic replies Alan had ever heard. On the verge of resigning himself to going back outside and listening to Wynn snoring in front of the TV set, Alan suddenly remembered the day he had pitched the Chicago Cubs to Casey Williams, shooting down all her objections over her desk without either of them opening their mouths. He had an intuition: Suppose he stopped worrying about what Judge Heinz clearly was never going to say and concentrated instead on listening to what the sot *wasn't* making audible? It was a momentous moment. Right away he picked up: "Leave me alone, jerk off," then something along the lines of "If I'd had you in my courtroom in my sober days . . ."

Alan needed all his self-restraint not to rejoice. But even as a hot flame of excitement speared his chest, he told himself he needed more, that his comprehension was coming too easily. So, as tactfully as he could, he asked Heinz if he had heard accurately. The judge appraised him even more balefully—now as a menace to some personal shelter he had been keeping within the municipal shelter. Before Alan could move, the old man sprang at his throat, digging his thumbs so hard into Alan's windpipe that, as he would subsequently joke, *all* his speech became omissive. In his fading consciousness he couldn't imagine anyone ever having to exercise his tongue or throat; indoor language was so much more wondrous in its ability to thrive whatever the emotional temperatures surrounding it.

Six months after Reggie Wynn and a couple of overnights had pulled Judge Heinz off him, Alan completed his first paper on what he copyrighted as Omissive Language. Two years after that, he managed to publish some of it on the OpEd page of the Hartford *Courant.* Reaction was instantaneous. Dozens of letters to the editor thanked him for translating into language a syndrome that had apparently been haunting a large segment of Connecticut. Wives expressed gratitude for having a new tool for dealing with taciturn husbands. Husbands said they were relieved not to have to respond vocally to illogical remarks and pointless observations. A police detective said he was confident the astute (and strictly Constitutional) use of omissive language would make it easier for law enforcement agencies to expose the lies of suspected perps during interrogations. On the other side of the fence, the president of the Connecticut Consumer Protection League worried in print that retailers would presume desires on the part of customers, making it more difficult for the latter to obtain refunds when charged for something not explicitly ordered. There were also warnings by the Danbury branch of the Sons of Italy that omissive language would increase incidents of Italian-American stereotyping. "We would have all been better off if this thing didn't exist," an organization communique lamented. "So as far as we're concerned, we'll continue to say just that—it doesn't exist. Anybody who says it does is embarked on an ethnic smear campaign that overlooks the social contributions of Mother Cabrini and Dean Martin."

Fortunately for Alan, one *Courant* reader who did subscribe to his insights was Hartford native Audrey Teller, a cousin of nuclear physicist Edward Teller and herself a tenured professor at Columbia University. Like her more famous cousin, who had spent most of his post-Hiroshima years warning about conspiracies not always obvious to the human senses, Audrey Teller was an expert in the hard-to-discern. Her particular forte was the history of the so-called Seven Wonders of the World—the Pyramids, the Hanging Gardens of Babylon, the statue of Zeus at Olympia, the Artemis temple at Ephesus, the Mausoleum at Halicarnassus, the Colossus of Rhodes, and the Pharos of Alexandria. Since only the Egyptian Pyramids had survived into modern times, she had fought more than one battle over the years not only defending the Seven as truly wondrous in their time, but also repudiating contentions that six of them might never have existed at all. It was in part thanks to these fractious experiences that she was able to reach out sympathetically to Alan, consoling him through doubts that his insights would ever produce cash; as far as she was concerned, she reassured him, omissive language was the eighth wonder of the world.

Despite the 28 years separating them, Alan fell dutifully in love with Audrey Teller. Not only did she admire him for the originality of his thought, she saw to it that her university board connections endorsed him as an instructor for the Psychology Department. The evening before his first class, he asked her to accompany him on a sentimental journey back to Municipal Inn #3. Standing across the street and watching the police vans unload their nightly catch for Reggie Wynn, he told her about how Matthew Pine had been the first to predict he would be a professor and how he felt as though he had carried through on an omissive commitment to the brewery's Vice-President for Popular Entertainment. Audrey said she understood, but mainly acted apprehensive about dawdling in her rings and bracelets in such a seedy neighborhood. He tuned out her caterwauling about wanting to get back to Hartford. The fact of the matter was, staring across the street at the dim lights of Municipal Inn #3, he couldn't believe he had once wanted to be sheltered. With his new job beckoning to him and the old lady pulling him back to her car, all that seemed so artificial to him now.

ARIZONA DIAMONDBACKS   (Mascot: Audrey Teller)

It took Alan years to be accepted by other members of Columbia's Psychology faculty. Those who didn't regard him as a flim-flam man personally fretted about the steady dilution of the behavioral sciences in the philistine interests of drawing more enrolments. At social events they treated their omissive language expert as they would have a waiter tardy about serving more Pinot Grigio. At faculty meetings his hand was usually left in the air so long an outsider might have mistaken his pose for that of somebody with an arm in traction. Nothing cheered his colleagues more than when a student dropped out of his class or complained that omissive language was a career track to a maintenance yard. Seldom did a month go by that some professor didn't go to the administration to protest what one termed "a creeping gimmickiness in analyzing the human vessel."

But Alan had his resources, too. First there was Audrey, whose relentless babbling about the Hanging Gardens after sex might have been wearing his patience thin but who never stopped working at shoring up his university position. At times, he felt as though all the Roman emperors combined couldn't have attended as many Classical History parties as she dragged him to, but it was through these social functions that he gained greater academic legitimacy— first from a Greek scholar who published a paper speculating on the omissive alibis of Demosthenes defending himself against charges of cowardice, then from an Hebraist who delivered a convention lecture on what had probably been going through Abraham's head in telling his son he had to go. It was because of this broadening interdisciplinary application of omissive language that *The New York Times* did a profile on Alan, concluding that there might not have been a final word yet on the relevance of his field of study, but that was all right until the paper could return to the subject in a year or so. Most important of all, in the ultimate repudiation of his backstabbing colleagues, every semester recorded a rise in the number of Omissive Language enrolments. As the university bursar reflected to Audrey during a fund-raising dinner: "The purists say we're watering down the product, but who cares as long as there's more product for more people?" Audrey took her cue and immediately began campaigning for Alan to be given full tenure.

When Alan did attain tenure, he thought of it as a spottled triumph. As part of a bureaucratic compromise, he had to share his moment of academic acknowledgement with Linda McElligott, a protege of the department chairman who had been conducting a course on Contemporary Hispanic Relationships for juniors and another on Contemporary Latino Relationships for seniors. In the interests of defusing the chairman's hostility to Alan's promotion, the university announced that McElligott's courses would thereafter be listed in the syllabus as Commissive Language Hispanic Style and Commissive Language Latino Style. It took Alan more than a few caresses from Audrey to accept this blatant exploitation of his pioneering work. Although McElligott, a tall redhead with white-on-white Irish skin, had been friendlier to him than most of his faculty colleagues, he was hard put to understand how somebody who was always doing samba steps in the teachers' room and going on about all the Bronx nightclubs she had closed at dawn could be confused with a serious psychologist.

His mood was tested further when, two days after banking the first check reflecting his more secure status at the university, Audrey rolled out of bed and didn't get up from the floor. The official finding was a weak heart, but Alan insisted to everyone the real cause had been stress. Linda McElligott was among the first to assume that Alan was blaming himself for Audrey's death, that he felt guilty about how she had spent her frail energies helping him get ahead. Alan was baffled to a frenzy of omissiveness when he grasped her insinuation. What he had been referring to, he allowed himself to verbalize to her at Audrey's funeral service in Hartford, was the old lady's exhaustion after so many years of reconstructing some goddamn thing called the Mausoleum at Halicarnassus. How could she have spent her life so morbidly? *Any*body outside a funeral director so preoccupied by dead Greeks who might not have even existed would have been stressed out.

When Audrey's will was read, Alan was disappointed to hear his name attached only to a collection of heavy, coffee table books with the Parthenon on the cover. On the other hand, as Linda McElligott reminded him at dinner the evening of the will reading, he could now throw off some of the emotional shadows he had picked up as Audrey's boy toy and reassert himself as his own free agent. Alan said that sounded great. What he didn't say was that he wouldn't have minded cha-cha-cha-ing right then and there with Linda McElligott to celebrate his new freedom. Happily for him, she overcame her commitment to commissive language to hear him.

10

BREAKTHROUGH

I N ANOTHER TESTAMENT to the recurrence of life's struggles, many of the labors Alan Gibb put in imposing Omissive Language were to be repeated a few years later with popularizing Franchisement. Sitting in his living room and crinkling the wrappers from his Jolly Ranchers, he still shakes his head at how he had to wander down some of the same new frontiers twice.

A lot of quacks will tell you they weren't new the second time because there had already been a first time. They're full of shit.

It's clear from his tone that he would prefer the questions to center more on Franchisement than on Omissive Language.

If I ask you how much money you have in your pocket, you going to start off telling me how many nickels and pennies you're carrying or run down the bills you have? Let's stay real here.

Following up on that theme, he reveals that once he had the ABCs of Franchisement in his head, he set to work recruiting the rest of the alphabet for the revolutionary manuscript to be known as *You're a Peewee, I'm a Bambino*. By his own account, he filled yellow legal pads with his tiny handwriting for 10 hours a day seven

days a week for the better part of two weeks. Hovering over his
labors was a growing premonition that he would be summoned at
any moment to the office of the department chairman for the news
that his omissive language classes were being dropped from the
curriculum. Linda McElligott's arguments that he was exaggerating
the precariousness of his situation fell on deaf ears; or better, he
wished he were deaf to them. But whenever she opened her mouth
to pooh-pooh his worries, he fell more deeply into the despair that
her yackety-yack was going to have the last word with the powers-
that-be, and very literally.

Some mystery has surrounded the sudden fears Gibb had for
his tenured position. They certainly didn't stem from enrolment
falloffs; on the contrary, he continued to be the biggest elective
draw in his department. If Audrey Teller's death had inevitably
made him less of a staple of board meeting conversation, it had
also come too late to undo all her persuasive work; he was in, and
that was all there was to it. Might his trepidations have been merely
a delayed reaction to his one-time involvement with the paranoid
Lenore Kindall? That has always seemed doubtful, though at least
one former city agency co-worker, Geronimo Morgan, has gone on
record as blaming Kindall for "infecting" him with the humorless
paranoia that led him to strangle a bus driver on Manhattan's
M10 line. (Morgan's defense was rejected by a murder jury.) Joel
Sternheim, the infomercials expert from Florida, has offered another
explanation:

> Everybody wants to make a quick buck. But to reach for the
> more, as I've always told my investment students, you have to
> keep an eye on the less for incentive. Nobody knows that more
> than Alan. He'd already piled up a few dollars with his omissive
> language business, but now he wanted to go further, rev up the
> engines for Franchisement. But how could he do that if omissive
> language represented a more, not a less, to him? So since he
> could hardly dispute his omissive language vision *in se*, he did
> the next best thing by attacking his ability to go on teaching it. At
> bottom, it was a risky investment in imagination.

Father Benjamin Acocella has gone further than Sternheim in the contention that, to be truly successful, Franchisement had to borrow some elements from omissive language and that Gibb's fears about losing his faculty position were merely an elaborate rationalization for pirating some of his source material from himself. Acocella:

> It's hardly a coincidence that both his worldviews call for diffident involvement by their direct subjects. Note, as well, how the same Alan Gibb has been the instigator of the two enterprises. You just cannot wake up one day and reinvent the wheel. As the Christians had to learn from the Jews and the ESTies from the Ponzi racket, you're always going to fall back on some basic elements from earlier versions of the Whole. Alan was building a yacht, he needed pieces from the rowboat he had been using, so he tried to cover it all up by saying the Psychology Department was plotting this mutiny against him.

Gibb has rejected such interpretations. While "I know what I know" has usually been the extent of his comment on the faculty termination fears, he has been at pains numerous times to ridicule any Franchisement debt to omissive language. As he complained to Jay Leno on the "Tonight" show during his promotion tour for *You're a Peewee, I'm a Bambino*:

> Forget Ebola fever. What terrifies people the most in this country is originality. It's like if they admit something is completely new, no debts to anything preceding it, that's jeering at your parents, "Ha, ha! I got here without you two getting it on!" Well, guess what, Mr. Leno? Franchisement *did* get here without any help from omissive language!

The truth would appear to fall somewhere in the middle. Omissive language and Franchisement clearly share several elements: a common ideator, a profound whimsicality in content analysis, and an optimism that anybody at all on the planet—American or foreigner, tall man or short woman—can be made subject to their plyings. But that said, there are also salient differences. The most marked of these is in the demand by Franchisement that customers speak up to say where they view themselves in the Personal Standings League, PITS, and Location options. Harvard's Jennifer Pryor is emphatic on this point:

> Omissive expression was embarrassment, tact, apprehension, and repressed hostility—what you might call non-thrust qualities. That is not the case with Franchisement, where you have the palpable human yearning to declare where you stand, to become more audible within an appropriate social framework, and to impregnate others with the seeds for judging one's performance.

Dr. Richard Toner, a Carnegie Foundation expert on metropolitan diseases and radical movements, agrees:

> I'm always wary of people like the Acocellas who insist there's nothing new under the sun. They're usually prime targets for skin cancer.

The hot debate around Franchisement's indebtedness to omissive language was still in the distance when Gibb completed his manuscript for *You're a Peewee, I'm a Bambino*. More immediate was the problem of getting his book to somebody who would know what to do with it. To test the waters, he showed it first to Linda McElligott. Although he had been dropping hints to her about his project for some time without being ridiculed, he was taken aback by her enthusiasm.

> A cynic might say she was just celebrating her victory. I was taking omissive language off the table, so she could now boast that her endless prattling relationships were the only ones to endure. Now that I had something new to focus on, she could rattle on forever about some Latino teaching assistant who, she said, had lied to her about some foster wife and foster kids in Chile. But because I'm not a cynic, I took her reaction as the

genuine article. Not only did she wish me happiness and luck, she predicted the book would purchase them for me.

McElligott:

I was bowled over. You have to remember I hate baseball. All those hand signs instead of stating openly what they want. But three pages into the manuscript, I sensed how far Alan had come. He had gotten over all his anxieties about people saying what was on their minds. Instead of that dread, a basic feature of omissive language, he had tapped an aching sweetness and found a profitable way to arrange it systematically.

McElligott also admitted to some personal ricochets from her reading of the book.

How could Franchisement theory not remind me of Julio, my Significant *Otro* at the time? Against the new charms of Alan, I had to face the fact that the only sweet thing about Julio was his body lotion. If he wasn't handing me his boots to shine, he was evading my questions about his Significant Otherettes down in Valparaiso. Ultimately, Franchisement saved me from that destructive relationship.

Buoyed by McElligott's response, Gibb circulated his manuscript among other academics who had never given him an especially hard time about omissive language. One of these was Abner Adams, a University of Tennessee scholar widely respected for his studies of fictitious folklore and manufactured myths. Adams:

I'd never been a fan of omissive language. I liked to joke that if he'd ever bothered taping the omissive swallowings of a goat, Gibb probably would have come up with a new State of the Union speech. My wife and I chuckled over that a lot. But I suppose because Gibb never actually heard me say that and because I was always polite to him at conventions and things, he'd jumped to the conclusion I was sympathetic to his work. As my

grandpappy used to say, that can lead to a lot of broken legs if
you choose the wrong riverbed at the wrong time of the year to
do your jumping. But fortunately, the book appealed to me in a
cowpatty way, so I got Rolf on the case.

Rolf was Randy Rolf, the New York editor of Adams's three
collections of tales and lies gathered from mountain communities
in Tennessee, Kentucky, and West Virginia. What Adams didn't
find out until later was that because the third of his collections had
done less than modestly, Rolf had been all but indifferent when she
received the manuscript for *You're a Peewee, I'm a Bambino* from
him, tossing it on a slush pile where it remained for two months.

They were months Gibb counted by minutes. He pestered
Adams so regularly that the folklorist called Rolf to disavow any
sponsorship of the manuscript (only to be told by Rolf's assistant
that the editor was in a meeting and couldn't speak to him). Finally,
while Adams was developing his own furies against his publisher,
Rolf called Gibb. Rolf:

> My most successful books had been a pictorial history of wrestling
> and a catalogue of popular nail polishes, so I was predisposed to
> both the sports motif and the all-inclusiveness of what Alan had
> set down. What I also saw right away were sweatshirt, calendar,
> and note block outlets for our marketing department.

As receptive as she was to *You're a Peewee, I'm a Bambino*, Rolf
had some editorial recommendations that Gibb balked at during
their first meeting at lunch.

> The lack of numbers bothered me. You need numbers attached
> to any characterology map. They make us feel closer to what an
> old sage called the infinite enigma. The Chinese, the Buddhists,
> the Incas—they all understood the power numbers have over the
> imagination and they shoved them in wherever possible. This
> one's lucky, that one's unlucky, that sort of thing.

When Gibb protested that numbers would serve only to evoke
baseball's obsession with statistics, thereby undermining his

efforts to play down Franchisement's relationship to the sport, Rolf noted that, lunch on her or not, they still didn't have a contract for the book.

> I wasn't proposing anything esoteric. All he had to do was
> figure out what numbers went best with a New York Yankee or
> Los Angeles Dodger personality, then list them. I told him I'd
> bet anything his followers would start to play those assigned
> numbers in things like state lotteries. And I also bet him we
> would all benefit from a promotion aftershock if a few of those
> numbers came up.

Rolf was proved correct. What ended up as Franchisement's Unique Numbers (FUN) brought the book invaluable publicity when a Cleveland Indians Personality from Butte and a St. Louis Cardinals Personality from Providence both parlayed their assigned numbers into appreciable lottery prizes. (Several other Franchisement customers would write to Gibb thanking him for using their FUNs to success in less official gambling games.)

Rolf's other major contribution to the manuscript was the addition of the Famous Franchise Folks (FFF). She has attributed this inspiration to her earlier work on the nail polish catalog. Rolf:

> It was my experience that the average career woman who leans
> toward, say, Raspberry Supreme gains greater self-worth if she
> knows Raspberry Supreme is also the favorite shade of Julia
> Roberts. You feel much closer to the "enamel network," as I
> have humorously designated it. I saw that Franchisement had
> the same potential. The Philadelphia Phillies or Atlanta Braves
> personality has to feel part of a bigger social picture if he knows
> he is going to be consulting the same charts as a Ricky Martin or
> Tom Brokaw.

Unlike his initial reaction to the FUNs, Gibb offered no resistance to buttressing his Personal Standings League identities with celebrities. As he noted in an email to Sidney Willinger following the publication of *You're a Peewee, I'm a Bambino*, he himself experienced a small thrill every year when he read over the list published by *USA Today* of actors, singers, and congressmen who shared his birthday. What he did hold out for, however, was that the FFFs not to be limited to the important people written about in gossip columns, but also include historical personages. This amendment made Randy Rolf the hesitant one.

> Like anybody cares what shade of nail polish Eleanor Roosevelt wore! Those old women always wore gloves, anyway! But he was adamant. No FFFs from the dawn of history and no book for my company. It was down to who was going to blink first.

> Rolf did.

> He wouldn't budge. If he couldn't have a dweeb like Ulysses Grant along with Madonna, he said he would take his project elsewhere. What else could I do except capitulate? I'd already gotten the wheels in motion on the sweatshirts and calendars. I didn't have any wiggle room.

Gibb and Rolf left their lunch fully agreed that the manuscript with the addition of the FUNs and FFFs would be in her office within a week. They also agreed that three weeks after that he would receive a check equal to his pay for four semesters of omissive language teaching. Did he feel completely triumphant? Or was there may be a trace of melancholy that, having accomplished his second worldview when the overwhelming majority of the planet's occupants couldn't manage even one, he didn't have anybody close to him to go out celebrating with? That Linda McElligott was with her Julio, that Abner Adams hadn't been all that much help anyway, that Teddy Doofle was dead—didn't this make his moment of greatest professional success somewhat bittersweet as he waited for the light to change at Fifth Avenue and 57th Street?

Gibb has heard the question before. Clutching his tea cup handle in the same hand as his Jolly Rancher wrappers, he emits a sigh for the ages. "Hell, no," he observes.

II

THE JOURNEY CONTINUES FURTHER STILL MORE

SAN FRANCISCO GIANTS (Mascot: Walter Luderus Again)

The last person Alan expected to be waiting for him outside his classroom one afternoon was Walter Luderus, the agent who decades earlier had conducted his high school class tour of the FBI building in Washington. But as if they had just spoken the day before, the still-emaciated if grayer Luderus twisted his jaw to say "Hello, Alan!" behind a firm handshake and then "You were right!" Before Alan could guess what he had been right about, Luderus guided him by the elbow down the hall toward the fire exit.

Standing on the fire steps, Alan was dumbfounded by what Luderus told him. Thanks to their conversation in the basement trophy hall, the agent explained, the Bureau had taken a closer look at the Puerto Rican problem, specifically as it related to one Gloria Tavarez. And although the investigation had yet to produce any prosecutable offense where Tavarez was concerned, it had led to a closer look at Alan's own circle. Had Alan been deliberately reticent about the activities of his stepfather Archie Geis? No matter; that was probably understandable. But there remained strong indications that, under the guise of driving the vehicles to prospective buyers who for one fictitious reason or another couldn't get down to his showroom, Geis had been using the GM products in his charge for private purposes for some time. The apparent complicity of fellow showroom workers over a great number of years elevated that crime to a conspiracy to defraud the American consumer.

Alan had an omissive thought ("You asshole, Archie retired months ago!"), but dropped it when Luderus, wiping perspiration off his hands with a handkerchief that was monogrammed WL-FBI-WASHINGTON, D.C., turned to his mother. Indeed, as Alan had probably meant to tip him years ago, the agent said, Louise Gibb had not been a model employee of the Board of Education. For one thing, there was her attitude toward minorities, which touched on civil rights abuses the Bureau was now obligated to worry about. More distressing, evidence compiled during three investigations pointed to Louise as a co-conspirator in a vast union featherbedding racket that had bled New York City of hundreds of millions of dollars, much of it in the area of instructional materials. While the Bureau regarded her as a relatively small (if bigoted) fish in a swampy pond, only her testimony against higher-ups in the racket would save her from a lengthy prison term. It wouldn't hurt, either, if she could name some of the people who had abetted her attitude toward blacks, Latins, and citizens of Asian persuasion.

Alan barely acknowledged the omissive greetings of the students passing up and down on the fire stairs. He was stunned by the implications of Luderus's news. Up to that moment, he had viewed his specialization only in terms of immediate and personal encoding and decoding; it had never occurred to him that what he had coined as the Comprehensible Unuttered (CU) could also span decades and miles, let alone spark enormous deployments of manpower for conducting the nation's business. Whatever other significance Luderus's information might have had, it was an astounding testimonial to how modest he had been in defining the parameters of omissive discourse.

Lying in bed that night in his West 112th Street furnished room, Alan brooded over the pros and cons of the situation with the millipede named Fred that had taken up quarters behind a print of the Golden Gate Bridge. If he did what Luderus advised, persuading his mother to testify against other custodians and racists, she would undoubtedly accuse him of being a rat; never again would she be able to count on his filial loyalty. On the other hand, he had to do something. What he finally decided, in the spirit of salvaging what was salvageable, was to leave her some pride by convincing her that squealing against other custodians would be the lesser evil to selling out her racist friends. He couldn't imagine Luderus objecting to that compromise.

He put his plan into action at a Sunday dinner at his mother's apartment. He kept his thoughts poised as Louise went on about how burdensome it was to have the retired Archie around the house 24 hours a day and Archie rhapsodized about moving out of the city to some sunnier climate in the southwest. Then, as Louise asked how Archie expected her to be able to collect her weekly paycheck from home if home was in another state, Alan trained all his thoughts into the objection that one federal prison looked like another. When the undeterred Archie replied that she had stashed away enough money and that he could find a showroom job anywhere, Alan refocused his thoughts on the reminder that serial borrowers could never hope to beat FBI circulars to a prospective employer. But nothing. Louise went back to pressing more roast beef and boiled potatoes on him, Archie kept talking about how convertibles were overrated in places like New Mexico, and both tried to act interested in "that sign language thing you teach."

When Louise and Archie were arrested on separate warrants a week later, Alan was distraught. The more Fred the millipede sought to console him that he had done his best to warn them, the more Alan was stupefied by the insufficiency of what until then had been his best. It was as if he had labored for years to build a house of cards in an unnatural calm, then had to watch it topple over before the first breeze: The conditions of his success, not the success itself, had been what was remarkable. Making a quick review of his life, he concluded that betrayal had been its major theme. His mother screwing with George Irvin on the couch and watching the Giants. His father standing him up at the Promenade. Lenore Kindall accusing him of being an industrial spy for Cincinnati. Gloria Tavarez never letting him go all the way. Matthew Pine coming through with merely a fraction of the bonus he had been promised. Audrey Teller leaving him nothing in her will except a lot of picture books about Greek statues. And the most perfidious traitor of them all? Who else but Alan Gibb, who had betrayed his own quest for originality (what had made Connie Theodore attracted to him) by settling for his stupid omissive language? Whatever Fred said to the contrary from the Golden Gate Bridge print, wasn't it obvious he had been pursuing betrayal willingly, gradually closing his silence around himself in the name of intellectual progress until the arrest of his mother and Archie signaled a final entrapment?

Linda McElligott refused to be so gloomy, saying that as long as he was ready to commit himself thoroughly to betrayal (she called it *traicion*) as part of his life design, he would be much healthier in his relationships. And a few weeks later, he did indeed find some room to delude himself that he was over the worst of his crisis. After a plea bargain deal, stipulating a suspended prison sentence and a fine equal to estimated compensation for all the gas and metallic wear he had been responsible for with his borrowed cars, Archie shrugged that he wasn't going to hold Alan's thoughts with Luderus against him, that it was part of the risk he had taken marrying Louise. As for Louise, her depositions on the custodial scam and her racist grandfather won her a reprieve while the FBI continued its investigations—time she spent being reborn as a Christian and accepting Jesus' wisdom that she had been as much of a rat as her son. When no grand jury indictments were forthcoming on either of the allegations against her after four years, she was given permission to move with Archie to Santa Fe.

Alan talked on and off about going to Santa Fe for a visit, but never got there. As he put it in words to Linda one night, "even China seems closer." Linda said she doubted that was true, but if that was where his emotions were geographically, he should chart his course appropriately. He thought he wished she would shut up.

LOS ANGELES DODGERS   (Mascot: Fred Gibb Still Again)

As protective as she was of her own discipline, Linda McElligott was alert to areas where Alan might reinforce his theories on omissive language. She urged him, for instance, to attend movies more regularly than was his habit, pointing out that they offered an opportunity to map scientifically the variety of communicative silences achieved through close-ups, two-shots, and Japanese actors portraying medieval peasants working rice paddies. At times her promptings embarrassed him, making him feel negligent about his own field of endeavor. For the most part, however, he interpreted her interest as a sincere attempt to broaden his perspectives so they would match the vast range of yackety-yack she thought of as her specialization. In his contemplative hours with Fred in his furnished room, he even gave himself over occasionally to the fantasy that, together, the two of them had *all* language covered. But that was a tinsel dream. As Fred seemed to enjoy reminding him, the more Linda helped him build up his lexicon of significant silences, the wider was the emotional gap between them. In her parlance, they gradually slipped down from being occasional lovers to being just *amigos*.

As for the movies Linda spurred him into seeing, Alan needed some time to get into sync with them. Especially when it came to new Hollywood productions, he found himself laughing at what the filmmakers had clearly intended as tragedy, grumbling over what they had deemed comic, and nodding off at what was supposed to have been thrilling. Over and over again—he radiated the thought to those around him—his orchestra seat was like a command cabin post on a spaceship that was blasting off toward its launching pad; the louder, smokier, and more orange things got in front of him, the more it became obvious that some basic planning flaw was making energies unfulfilled.

Still, he got into the habit of dropping by his neighborhood multiplex at least once a week. And once over being distracted by the action and dialogue on the screen, he came to see that the salient omissive experience of movie-going wasn't the unarticulated speech of the characters, but rather the implicit messages being sent by the film makers. Some of the more frequent of these unheard utterances, as he reported to his students, were:

"What do you think of this shit?"
"Bet you regret opening your wallet now."
"You want logic, read a philosophy book."

So much negativity truly dispirited him. He had never suspected that omissive discourse was radically different from other communication means in its proportions of benevolence and malevolence. But rarely was he able to enter his class Monday morning to say he had seen a film over the weekend containing totally positive insinuations. He dropped into a crisis even deeper than that after the arrests of Louise and Archie because this time the very pylons of his intellectual originality felt under siege. Was it possible only his own sanguine outlook had been giving the best of it to all the other readings he had been making of people since Judge Heinz? The thought alone made him feel cheesy. The structures of the success he had built up from Matthew Pine to Audrey Teller began swaying above the tremors of his self-doubt. Even Fred mocked his reflections. He took care of the bug by swatting it with a *Daily News*, but his self-confidence wasn't restored so easily. Once he himself began questioning the substance of omissive language, wasn't the emperor truly bare-assed for all to see? Suddenly, it seemed like only a matter of time before parents began protesting how they were spending their tuition money, the university decided it needed fresher enrolment gimmicks, and he needed a new job.

Then what Cassandra Williams would have marketed as a miracle happened. Increasingly anxious over the loquacious looks his students were giving him, Alan cancelled a week of classes with the excuse of being ill. It wasn't that much of an exaggeration since he spent the week wallowing in the movie houses that had triggered his enervating fever. Like a crazed crack addict doubling his intake from one day to the next, he stumbled from theater to theater around the city, gorging himself with as many as four pictures between noon and midnight. What any one of them was about he barely recalled two movies later, and didn't feel the loss. What they were all about, he didn't feel the need to point out to the senior citizens clustered around him for the afternoon shows, was Alan Gibb.

Then he paid his way in to see an Australian feature entitled *Twilight of the American Salesman*. *Twilight of the American Salesman* was about a traveling salesman named Willie who can't wait to get away from his morose wife and two dimwit sons and get back out on the road where he has been organizing orgies for years. Only when Willie contracts syphilis does he discover that everybody—his wife, his sons, his employer—would have shaken him loose a long time before if not for his absences for selling women's hosiery out of town. Once he tells them about the venereal disease that will keep him housebound, they all beat it—the wife to a gold miner named Jock, one son to a male exotic dancer in Perth, the other to a job with a supermarket tabloid in New Zealand, and his employer to Fiji. Willie, whose maternal grandfather had worked for Henry Ford in Michigan, is left alone on his couch lamenting the end of the American Dream.

As he would confide later, Alan didn't need any special reasons for being moved by *Twilight of the American Salesman*. The title alone had been reopening his old wounds about Fred Gibb walking out on him after their day at Ebbets Field and then standing him up at the Promenade. But there was a special reason, anyway. It came in a party scene where Willie was showing off his hookers to other salesmen in a motel room. It took Alan a long moment to recognize Fred Gibb. As in the #7 train years before, he had the fluttering sensation of being a second or two behind somebody recognizing him first. The face peering out at him from the screen was of the quintessential extra—an elderly man with a big gut, wearing a paper party hat, holding a glass of amber liquid in one hand and trying to look natural about smooching with the mini-skirted redhead on his lap. Fred's first omissive cry was "See—authenticity!" since the filmmakers had apparently gone out of their way to find real traveling salesmen for the scene. The second was "Hi, Alan! It's me, your old Dad!"

Alan's reply died in his throat, not even rising to omissive level. He was too overwhelmed to care whether he was yelling verbals or merely oozing them. Had he overrated, underrated, or not rated at all the paunchy man staring down at him from the screen with a lecherous twinkle? When last heard about, his father had been peddling knapsacks in New Jersey, but he saw no sign of spine curvature. How could he have imagined Fred Gibb—a failure even at Samsonite luggage—being capable of crossing the rest of the country and the Pacific Ocean and cutting himself into the most glamorous of all mass media? On the other hand, he was dismayed his father could have traveled as far as Australia at the sacrifice of so much merely to end up going "Har-har-har, come here, sweetie" for a sleazy production like *Twilight of the American Salesman*. Had that been in his dreams when he had dumped his son home after their last game at Ebbets Field? The third hand? He was staring back at the old man on the screen like any other spectator in the movie house. All the personal resentments and genetic prides that had been driving him for years seemed to have dissolved in his soul. Fred Gibb had turned into just one more anonymous onlooker for Alan Gibb's journey.

It was a devastating moment. If Alan could no longer rely even on his ensnarled omissive feelings for his father to supply fuel for his omissive language insights, what could he trust? The emperor wasn't only naked, he was an X-ray. Clearly, the time had come to be more original in some more dependable, less personal way than omissive language provided.

It was the following week, returning to Columbia after his declared illness, that Alan Gibb went to the bus stop at Broadway and West 76th Street and encountered the small boy dressed in contradictory clothing.

12

FRANCHISEMENT'S F WORDS

ALAN GIBB WAS tempted to throw down any numbers at all to get Randy Rolf off his back and *You're a Peewee, I'm a Bambino* off the presses. But he couldn't do it. As hard as it was for him to credit anything proposed by his editor, he couldn't turn away from the vast ocean of numbers she had forced him to look at—more of them, actually, than the customers of his wildest hopes. As he noted to Linda McElligott, there were even more numbers for helping define his customers than there were numbers themselves since some of them could be applied to more than one Franchisement personality. What Franchisement's Unique Numbers (FUN) amounted to, he pointed out to her, was something more infinite than traditional infinity itself.

However that might be, he set about wringing potential significances out of the basic integers (0 through 9) and their assorted couplings, triplings, and the rest. There were moments of exhilaration during his labors in his Columbus Avenue furnished room when he felt like a child making, unmaking, and remaking sand pies on the beach. Every time logic's waves washed in to crumple his work, he wanted to squeal with delight and chase them back out to their relentless source. In Franchisement's own terms, he realized, he was enjoying the benefits of Location, feeling only FREE and JOYOUS at his task.

The ultimate FUN, he had little problem deciding, was 16—the number of franchises in the Personal Standings League and the number that had informed so much of his earliest inspiration and research. It was the ace in poker, 100 in a school grade, and 10 in evaluating the worth of physical graces. 16 stood responsive to any and all—perfectly divisible by both individual integer and square root, composed of a stern digit and a cuddly one, flexible enough for a different FUN value when turned upside down. Excluding harassed parents who found nothing sweet about a daughter reaching that age, 16 was TOTALLY POSITIVE.

While 16 had no converse (since NOTHING COULD BE TOTALLY NEGATIVE), Gibb needed little reflection to be wary of 0. Even ignoring its historical associations with the hopeless, bankrupt, and nihilistic, he shuddered before its self-containment, its circular claustrophobia, and its ambiguous relationship with the alphabet. *In se* zero gave nothing and mocked everything. More often than not, even its usefulness was parasitic—flanking other numerals for their ostensible empowerment but in reality for its own. It was, in short, an addend that defied the personality to reach a sum.

Outlining the general characters of 16, 0, and other numbers was, of course, the easiest part of Gibb's computations. Far more arduous was setting them within the context of the Personal Standings League as influenced by the PITS and Location; i.e., calculating the particular weight of a number vis-a-vis the given customer. A 7 that intimated a stock portfolio bonanza for a Houston Astros Personality with a Pitching PITS might, in the case of a Houston Astros Personality with a Running PITS, suggest the wisdom of unloading the portfolio as soon as possible. The Los Angeles Dodgers Personality with a Fielding PITS who concluded that his personal FUN of 111 meant he should take Delta flight 111 on a business trip, might risk crashing into the Rockies if he had a Hitting PITS. At issue wasn't the common interpretative reassurance given to both customers that they would survive the crash in any case; the point was that only the most meticulous charting of a FUN in relation to customized Personal Standings League and PITS choices could spare the unluckier of the two passengers panic in the cabin as the plane lost altitude, a bump on the head when the craft bellied into the mountain, and long days of hypothermia, hunger, and difficult moral culinary choices in the snow while waiting for rescue teams to arrive.

Gibb has always been reluctant to discuss the mechanism he came up with for assuring this integration. Pressed by interviewers and customers alike, he has usually hidden behind drolleries such as "Next you'll expect Coca-Cola to tell you its secret formula." Incontrovertible, however, has been FUN's plausible illumination and reinforcement of the basic character tendencies indicated by Personal Standings League and PITS choices. Jack Fenaughty, an admitted skeptic when he submitted to his first Franchisement reading, has offered one testimonial among thousands. As the Wall Street analyst recalls:

> I phoned their 900 number just to get a whiff, to see if the rumblings I'd been hearing were a financial quake in the making or the normal burps for another novelty here today and gone tomorrow. The woman on the phone sounded like she'd once worked for one of those suicide centers. You know, "Let's all feel sorry for ourselves while we keep the meter ticking to show you how much living is going to cost you." I told her I was a New York Yankees Personality because I steamroller to the bottom line. She's all oh-yes-this and oh-yes-that. I'm about to hang up figuring another con game that'll be chased up the block the next day, but then she suddenly starts hitting me with things she couldn't possibly have gotten from our little talk. First she typed me as a Pitching PITS. No one knew that. They all think of me as the classic Hitting PITS. But number one, I'm a team guy, number one-and-a-half, I'm a dominant team guy.

And his FUN?

> That's what really knocked me out. I told her, I said, "My first number is 1,000,006. Bet you don't know why." She didn't lose

a second! "That's very appropriate, Mr. Fenaughty," she says. "You've wanted to be a millionaire since childhood, but you've also always wanted to have a few dollars in addition to that so you could joke to all your friends you weren't *just* a millionaire." That was it exactly! She even knew I wanted only those six bucks more because any more and I would've jumped into another tax bracket. Believe me, when they say the FUN number is important, they're not talking through their hats.

Another witness to the crucial nature of FUN was Karen Goldensohn, a computer repair manager in Austin. After more than a year of accepting her status as a St. Louis Cardinals Personality with a Fielding PITS and FUN numbers of 0, 1, and 10, Goldensohn called the Franchisement hotline for another reading.

I'd been in a rut for more than a year. Okay, I had accepted I was the kind of person who was better off blaming others for my shortcomings. Why not? That gave me more personal space to explore other possible flaws. But that wasn't doing the job. When I asked them to give me a new franchise, though, I heard the hesitation in the counselor's voice. I reminded her that was part of the deal, changing whenever I felt like it. She couldn't have been nicer. "Of course," she said. "I can give you a new franchise at once. But are you really certain that's what you want to do? Because by changing your franchise, you're in effect blaming the St. Louis Cardinals typology for your troubles. In other words, you're admitting how much a Cardinals Personality you really are." It was true, of course, and I felt lost. But then she told me the solution.

It turned out to be a simple adjustment in Goldensohn's FUN.

We kept the Cardinals and the Fielding PITS. The trouble, we agreed, was in my FUN numbers of 0, 1, and 10. Unconsciously, I'd been taking my computer job home with me every night. Sure, I felt like I was in a rut, because I was! So we changed my FUN to 25, 85, and 123.

More than a year after the fact, Goldensohn cannot contain a joyful giggle over the consequences of that small modification.

> Two days later, I was summoned to the office of the director and told I was being promoted. Instead of the 25 people who had been under me to that point, I was now head of 85!

That explained the 25 and 85 of her choice, but what about the 123? On this point, Goldensohn adopts a more tactful tone.

> Well, I guess you could look at the company payroll and see that, including me, we have 124 employees. That, of course, would drop to 123 if I got that prick director's job and kicked his ass out the door.

To his credit, Gibb has never affected surprise over such success stories. For one thing, he has long since dismissed Randy Rolf's importance in the formulation of FUN ("Any passerby can tell you where the bus stop is, but you're the one who has to pay the fare and take the ride."). For another, he knows that with such an inexhaustible supply of numbers at his disposal, he will always be able to make the appropriate matches for customers. As he phrased it in *You're a Peewee, I'm a Bambino*:

> There's something eerie, in a positive way, how FUN can be so much fun.

Father Benjamin Acocella has noticed the same thing. As he told his ecumenical council at the session that formally welcomed Franchisement as a member:

> It goes generally unremarked that one of the most precious achievements of Franchisement has been the restoration of the fabled *homo ludens*—the playful soul living in the lap of God, Kali, and Ethical Culture, innocent and humble even in his cunning, aware that, however slack the leash around his throat, he will one day be yanked back to the Great Giver of All

Games. With FUN, especially, Franchisement blends the finite and the infinite into the nectar that will always be both—HUMAN HAPPINESS.

FFF

If Gibb needed a few minutes to call FUN his own, he didn't wait even that long to expropriate Randy Rolf's other recommendation of celebrity Franchisement types. He hadn't been bluffing, either, with his insistence on including historical figures. As he told *Entertainment Weekly* in March 2000:

> Just because Franchisement itself owes nothing to the past
> doesn't mean you can't borrow some useful things every once in a
> while. The more you drag things from the past up to the present,
> in fact, the more you're going to be showing how that past would
> have been lots better off being where we are. That goes for a lot of
> old dead people, too.

As in the case of FUN, the FFFs (Famous Franchisement Folks) offered Gibb a vista without confines. He didn't have to consult almanacs or history books to gauge into the millions the number of people who had made a significant contribution to the development of the human race. Any tabloid newspaper, cable TV station, or website provided innumerable examples of unknowns who were regarded as modern celebrities. Throwing both groups into one pool, Gibb would be quoted by Sidney Willinger as saying, was "like creating a tsunami of candidates."

He set to the task of straining the pool. His first criterion was that the FFFs had to have accomplished something POSITIVE with their lives, and not merely by indirection. Thus, he could eliminate right away the likes of Adolf Hitler, Typhoid Mary, and Don Ho. His second criterion was the exclusion of those who, while clearly corresponding to a given franchise characterology (e.g., Cain with the Philadelphia Phillies, Saint Sebastian with the Chicago Cubs), declined to open themselves to the contradictions and enrichments brought by a PITS or a FUN. For Gibb, these single-track figures recalled the simplistic mode of horoscopy in which "a Capricorn was a goat and only a goat—to nobody's benefit or progressive complexity." No more welcome, he stipulated, were those who would appear to claim some practical lien on a given selection in the Personality Standings League; for example, a Bob Hope defined as a Cleveland Indians Personality just because the comedian had once owned part of the team. Rather than go through lengthy explanations about why a Hope was actually a Boston Red Sox Personality, perhaps alienating some of his geriatric fans in the process, such Famous Figures would be siphoned out of the pool from the outset.

As for the specific factors determining his assignment of FFFs to given typologies, Gibb has been as elusive on this as he has been on the subject of Franchisement's Unique Numbers. "Next thing you'll want to know is who really killed the Kennedys," as he smiled enigmatically to Ted Koppel after being asked that question. Again, though, his accuracy has been undeniable, and has made it easier for even the most exasperated customer to stay on the line in expectation of a new, personal link to the past. Typical has been the case of Harris Heim, a Long Island antiques dealer. Heim:

> They pulled me through a dozen franchises to find a reading that didn't say I was a *schlemiel* buying Korean rip-offs as authentic Tiffany. We finally settled on a Raincheck PITS for the San Francisco Giants. My key, the woman on the phone kept saying, was that I was the kind of a guy who saved his best for last. If I wasn't in a hole for $100 already, I would've made slamming the phone down in her ear my best for last. But as soon as she started talking about some of the famous people in my category, I was glad I'd hung in there.

Who were some of the FFFs who shared Harris Heim's reading as a San Francisco Giant with a Raincheck PITS?

> The one that got to me right away was that Icarus. Okay, he wasn't so old when he got to his last and he never got where he

wanted to go. But he had the guts of a burglar and he was going
after something that even now today would be a helluva lot better
than the airplane or the helicopter. I took that as one big omen
that maybe I should take a flyer of my own. So I quit worrying
about the authenticity of every goddamn piece of glass I picked
up at flea markets and just unloaded it. I like thinking even
Icarus is up there saying *caveat emptor*.

Equally affected by the FFFs was Gladys Shea, a Cincinnati
cocktail waitress and single mother of two. As Shea told an ESPN
documentary on the successes of Franchisement's first three years:

I share my Franchisement identity with Cher and Clara Barton,
and I need both. Barton makes me remember that instead of
griping about the animals I have to serve every day or how the
kids always want more than I can give them, I ought to remember
the wretched people around the world who'd die to be in my
situation. Cher works the opposite effect on me. I want to be
out there flaunting it and shaking it all the time. Together, they
make me feel I've got everything covered—from self-pity to self-
confidence. What else can I ask from a self?

Gibb's own answer to that came during a question-and-
answer session at the Foreign Press Club in Washington in March
1999. Asked by a reporter from the Copenhagen daily *Politiken* if
Franchisement's very SUCCESS didn't imply a ceiling, floor, and four
walls around human potential, he noted how, in the area of FFFs
alone, he had come nowhere near exhausting association models.
"A customer of ours named Gladys Shea once asked rhetorically
what more she could ask of a self," Gibb said patiently to the Danish
newsman. "The answer to that, of course, is everything she has yet
to ask. Franchisement is an open-minded business."

13

CAPITAL GAINS
AND
HEALTH GAINS

SKEPTICS HAVE COMPARED the publication of *You're a Peewee, I'm a Bambino* to the marketing of Hula Hoops, Pet Rocks, and Cabbage Patch Dolls. Other commentators have likened the phenomenon to the Chinese actually paying for copies of Mao's Thoughts or to guests paying for hotel room Bibles. Perhaps the show business weekly *Variety* characterized the explosion most succinctly with its headline of FRANCHIE FRENCH KISSES AMERICA.

Even Randy Rolf has admitted not being quite prepared for the public response. As she reminisced in her memoir *Randy Rolf Unedited*:

> I really thought the calendars, sweatshirts, and notepads would
> cover it. To get even that much through Marketing almost
> cost me my virginity (hohoho). They had this Pavlovian way of
> merchandising; to wit, do it the way it had already been done.

John Updike had moved only bookmarks, so that was all Alan
Gibb could move. One of those bitter old Irish bores had moved
only a plastic potato, so that was all Alan Gibb would be able to
move. But a week after we hit the bookstores, the warehouses
were calling in a panic that they'd even run out of the calendars
and shirts! What were we going to do? I'd underestimated my
success.

There has been divided opinion about what catapulted *You're a
Peewee, I'm a Bambino* from the ranks of a general reference book
on human behavior to the popular cultural assumption we know it
as today. Pundits agree, however, that five factors have been pivotal
to one degree or another:

1. The mugging of Alan Gibb in Riverside Park. After leaving Linda
McElligott off in front of her Riverside Drive apartment one night,
Gibb decided the weather was balmy enough for a stroll in the
park. Three blocks along, he was slugged from behind and sent
reeling into a park bench painted with bird droppings. His first
thought, as he would confess later, was that Irony was afoot, since
the earlier attack on him and Father Acocella in Central Park had
coincided with his vision of the Location principle. Was he about to
lose everything in the same manner he had gained everything? But
before he had to probe that question to any degree, two teenagers
passing by came to his rescue, overpowering the mugger and calling
for the police. All the way over to the station house, the dazed Gibb
tried to remember where he had seen the now-handcuffed mugger
before. Only when TV camera crews began descending on the
precinct did he get it out of a desk sergeant that his assailant was a
recently deposed Schools Chancellor for New York City. According
to the sergeant, the former official had not only fallen on lean times
personally, but had resorted to his desperate attack to dramatize
the budget crisis in the city's public education system.

Inevitably, there was huge media coverage of the attempted
mugging, and Gibb never missed an opportunity to sneak in a
commercial for his soon-to-be-published book. In Randy Rolf's
words, "Alan's exploitation of the situation created more expectation

than we had a right to expect. We also had the tragedy angle in that he had been brutalized by somebody who had once probably signed off on his mother's unearned checks. There was a double violation in that which seemed to hit home with a lot of people."

2. Little promotional competition. As enthusiastic as she was about *You're a Peewee, I'm a Bambino*, Randy Rolf was only too aware that its publication figured to be overshadowed even within her own house by the simultaneous appearance of a new Tom Clancy novel. But at the eleventh hour, following charges from the U.S. Navy that the "novel" was actually a copy of official contingency plans for invading Trinidad and Tobago, the publisher had to withdraw Clancy's book, freeing up millions of dollars in promotion money for Gibb's work. Overnight, Gibb found himself booked for flights and TV programs from one end of the country to the other, not only fulfilling Clancy's commitments but trying to distract attention from the outrage emanating from Port-of-Spain and spreading across the Caribbean.

3. The Gibb appeal. All the promotional efforts would have been in vain if Gibb hadn't succeeded in tapping a responsive chord in the American public. In fact, he proved to be a persuasive, sympathetic figure. Randolph Cotton, marketing director for the publishing house, described his TV appearances as those of "a frightened little kid who keeps bouncing up and down on the couch, afraid he'll slip under the cushions, all the time imploring the adults around him to listen before the whole house burns down."

Syndicated columnist Jimmy Breslin put it this way: "Gibb is the break-your-heart latchkey kid who runs down to the OTB to beg his old man to help him find his lost kitten and doesn't want to hear the old man is more interested in what's running at the Seventh at Belmont. The kid knows better than the father that the City Hall scum mean it literally when they say they're going to give the poor of this city cat food to eat and he needs the old man to help him out before the animal catcher shows up. You don't help this kid right away, you deserve to stand in a swamp of cigarette butts and tout sheets tearing up your tickets for the next 20 years."

The first measure of Gibb's ability to get across was in the volume of emails and phone calls to the stations that had him on as a guest. On the Pittsburgh morning show "Here We Go Again," his appearance elicited 3,200 e-mails within three hours (the phone calls stopped being counted after overworked operators protested). In what quickly became a nationwide pattern, the respondents not only requested more information about the basics of Franchisement, but volunteered their own impressions of what typologies they represented. Leisure scientist Sidney Willinger, for one, saw this as an early sign that *You're a Peewee, I'm a Bambino* was destined to be more than just another mental fitness tome seeking readers. Willinger:

> So many leisure activities are essentially monologues. You may talk trash with your pals as you bowl or shoot pool, but the principal conversation is between you and your balls. You go out jogging with your lover, but every breath you waste on each other means so much less ground covered. You sit at home with your family watching the tube, but every time somebody opens his yap, you have to shush him or miss a key plot development. Franchisement, on the other hand, offered dialogue, and the country couldn't say enough.

4. *Influential backers.* Just as Audrey Teller was indispensable to him for draping omissive language with academic respectability, Gibb found a powerful angel for Franchisement in Bart Patterson. Founder of the Oakland-based Patterson Information Systems and a multimillionaire at 23, Patterson had spent the decade before encountering Gibb doing business penance for the first source of his wealth—a 666 line that had enjoyed a vogue in the 1980s among cultists anxious for up-to-date reports on Satan's imminent ascension. When one of his regular callers (revealed as having spent $4,500 monthly on the 666 line) walked into a Burger King in Lima, Ohio and slaughtered 21 people in the name of "speeding along the Master's arrival," Patterson was shamed into discontinuing his entertainment service. He thereupon embarked on a series of investment ventures aimed at (as he told *Business Week* in November

1989) "restoring the good and the healthy to the American mind." He made even more money from these undertakings, which included a 999 number that brought callers reassurances that angels were ready to defend them against Satan's armies. For three years in a row, he was given the 73rd slot in the Fortune 500 list.

So what could Franchisement give Bart Patterson that he didn't already have? Patterson:

> This guy Gibb was pitching GOOD THINGS FOR EVERYBODY, and you can never have enough GOOD THINGS FOR EVERYBODY. For once we had a GOOD SHEPHERD, not the usual zombie feeding his followers cyanide before the big meeting in the sky with Zombie Supremo.

Thanks to Patterson's in-place facilities, Gibb was able to make a 900-FRANCHLY line operational even before ending his book publicity tour. Under terms of the deal, Patterson and a newly created Franchisement Enterprises divided the proceeds evenly, with Patterson assuming all the expenses for technical overhead and Gibb paying for the training and staffing of the 24-hour counselor-operators and promotional advertising. (There was instant agreement between the sides that customer contact would be made solely through the telephone, computer communication regarded as too impersonal.) Within six months, the business was averaging 9,000 calls a day; after two years, it declared a profit of $36.5 million. Like Randy Rolf, Patterson was taken aback by the dimensions of Franchisement's success. As he quipped to *Money* magazine in 1995: "We were so busy taking it in hand over fist, we needed more hands and fists."

5. *The Surgeon-General's report.* Its initial success notwithstanding, Franchisement might have remained a transient phenomenon if not for "The Surgeon-General's Biweekly Report on Cancer and Anti-Cancer Surrogates," issued in the immediate wake of the commencement of 900-FRANCHLY's operations. Although accounting for less than a page in a document that ran to 1,200 pages, the report's praise of Franchisement as a barrier to cancer

became front-page news all over the country. In the words of the government document:

> The panel is unanimous in its finding that no stronger force against cancer exists than the so-called human mind, being understood in this concept both emotional and ideational impulses. Sufficient testimony has been rendered to the panel for a conclusion that, even if invisible outside its cranial envelope, the mind exerts a formidable defensive influence on visible humors and systems, bringing assets (including confidence, determination, and strength of purpose) not customarily available to organs, joints, and bones. However notional some of these assets, they have proven in cases studied by the panel to have been decisive in staunching tumors, there simply being no rival explanation for the physical reversals witnessed. It should be noted in this context that adepts of the recent value system Franchisement have shown particularly strong defenses against corporeal debilities of an oncogenous nature. Pending any contradictory evidence, the panel has concluded that Franchisement plays an immunological role more palpable than any other mental system familiar to its members.

For an official government report, the language conveying the findings of the Surgeon-General on Franchisement was unusually forthright, and probably would have caused considerable commentary anyway. But thanks to Franchisement's public relations machinery, the document's praise of Gibb's vision became a fireball screaming through the media. If the *Daily News* was the first, it was far from being the only paper to use the headline FRAN FANS CANCER. Even cautionary notes sounded in editorials in such dailies as the Washington *Post* and San Francisco *Chronicle* mainly conveyed the sense of editorial writers trying to contain their excitement because they didn't want to risk being mocked by history books a hundred years after the fact. Within weeks, nine prime-time television magazine shows devoted segments to Franchisement, the history of non-medical cures for cancer, or alleged links between Franchisement and members of the Surgeon-General's panel (two surgeons and a heart specialist were revealed as 900-FRANCHLY subscribers, but none had a financial stake in the company). As symptomatic as anything, Franchisement came in for mockery in comedy monologues, while Gibb himself was impersonated regularly on "Saturday Night Live," usually as a teething baseball fan in the grandstand slopping mustard all over his shirt in the middle of lectures to fellow spectators on such arcane subjects as the War of the Roses and duckpin bowling. When even the President of the United States was disclosed as having pressed a copy of *You're a Peewee, I'm a Bambino* on a son arrested for drag racing on Pennsylvania Avenue, nobody could deny that the vision that had loomed into view on Broadway and West 76th Street shortly after 2:00 P.M. on July 16, 1991 had attained an institutional status.

14

OUT OF THE PAST

THE TIDAL WAVE answering to the name of Franchisement could hardly leave Alan Gibb dry personally. The least of it was the necessity of resigning from Columbia to have more time to devote to his new enterprise. Given his earlier anxieties about being fired, this wasn't a step without its satisfactions, and in succeeding years he often regaled intimates with the scene of walking into the office of his department chairman, handing over his resignation letter, and announcing that "omissive language just doesn't say enough to me anymore." Otherwise, however, his first months in the wake of *You're a Peewee, I'm a Bambino* were, by his own admission, disorienting. Even now, as he frowns at the appearance of a purple Jolly Rancher in his hand, he can say: "You get used to things. Good, bad, or indifferent, they're things. When they weren't there anymore, I couldn't keep used to them."

First there was his break with Linda McElligott. As much of a friend as he had had since Teddy Doofle, McElligott took his resignation from teaching badly. As she explained it, she simply wasn't prepared for the new kind of "structured relationship" his absence from the campus would dictate. When he asked what she meant by that, she pointed out they would now need to phone or email one another even just to arrange a coffee together. He couldn't deny that, but then reminded her she would be freer to say no to him at a distance than she had been walking down a university corridor with him. For reasons utterly unfathomable to Alan, this triggered a barrage of charges that he had always been jealous of Julio, Carlos, and her other lovers—not only because of sex, but because she had always been able to use her commissive language in Spanish as much as in English. The flabbergasted Gibb had no response to that in either tongue. Then he made what turned out to be a bigger gaffe by offering to do her Franchisement chart gratis. McElligott:

> He really believed you could categorize human beings according to some neat phrases—as if he didn't know every word we say to each other contradicts the one we just finished saying! I didn't know whether to laugh or to cry, so I did both. After all our years together, the ups and the downs, the unders and the overs, all he could think to do was draw me into this game of his. Had we ever truly communicated in any serious way? Where was the *respeto*?

Although McElligott would temper her attitude toward Gibb and the Franchisement theory later on, her estrangement in the period immediately following the publication of *I'm a Peewee, You're a Bambino* opened a "vacuum in (the) heart" of the Father of Franchisement as he went shopping for that item and other household things. The need to move out of his Columbus Avenue furnished room into a three-room apartment on Central Park West, as he has written, "left me feeling like the most impractical person in the world. I would enter stores looking for chairs, crockery, or silverware and I would be omissively asking Linda which ones I should choose. Instead of having her there with her experience in these matters, I had salespeople sizing up this 52-year-old as somebody taking his first steps out of the playpen and talking to me like if I picked the most expensive items, they'd give me a lollipop."

The publicity generated by Franchisement also brought numerous unwelcome calls and visitors from past stop-offs on the Journey. One was Archie Geis, who phoned from Santa Fe to wonder aloud whether the constant refundability of Franchisement's readings hadn't been inspired by his cavalier ways with GM vehicles, entitling him to a piece of the profits. Archie was reminded that, unlike his activities, Franchisement was not illegal. Conceding this was probably an important difference, the retired salesman said goodbye and put Louise on the phone. For her part, Louise said she didn't know what was so new about New Mexico if there were Mexicans every place she looked. Alan's reminder to her was that she had barely gotten off the last time on her racist views and that, if her telephone was tapped, she might not be so lucky the second time. Louise thanked him for the heads up and hung up.

Matthew Pine wasn't so easy to get rid of. Returning home one evening from a Waldorf banquet honoring Bart Patterson's contributions to the Ecumenical Council on Mental Observances, Gibb found the former brewery executive sprawled out drunk on the sidewalk in front of his building. Telling the doorman to cancel a call to the police, he helped Pine up to his apartment and force-fed him some coffee. A more coherent Pine told him more than he wanted to know: he had been fired from the brewery for going back on the sauce, he had lost all his savings in a vain attempt to sue the brewery for intoxicating the country with its chemical additives, and he had even been tossed out of Municipal Inn #214 for assaulting another overnight. As he summed it up for Gibb: "I'm coasting aloft here in my glider, Alan. But I got the Zeros on one side and the MIGs on the other, and the only way to get away from them is to dive right into the smokestacks of the carrier *U.S.S. Instant Death*. What does Franchisement say about that, buddy?"

In fact, it said Chicago Cubs Personality with a Fielding PITS, but rather than try to explain that to Pine in his woozy state, Gibb mentally ran down the employment possibilities within Franchisement suited to his former boss's abilities. Did he owe Matthew Pine anything? The one thing he could think of was the fame he had gained from the beer commercial. Much longer, it seemed, was the list of what he *should* have owed him—the big cash bonus (instead of the measly $350 he had received), use of his consultancy title at the brewery (instead of never having been called again), and success with Cassandra Williams (instead of having been blackmailed into ruin). In the end, therefore, he sent Pine on his way with $20 and warned the doorman never to let him in again.

He also could have done without a reappearance by Theodore Herzl, his one-time classmate who had become a highly publicized community leader in the Crown Heights section of Brooklyn. For Herzl, Franchisement was only another godless attempt to divert attention from keeping the state of Israel strong against its enemies, and hardly a week passed that the diamond dealer wasn't being quoted somewhere denouncing "cartoon minds that should be dragged into the streets and have their blasphemous limbs pulled off." Although the screeds had the commercial effect of winning customers for Franchisement among Herzl's black and Latin opponents in Brooklyn, anti-Semites across the country, and several members of the British House of Lords and the French Academy, Gibb did not entertain illusions: The negativity could only boomerang against his enterprise in the long run. Thus, he arranged a hush-hush meeting with Herzl at the Prospect Park Zoo to defuse the situation.

When the Hasid showed up with more than 30 followers, Gibb feared his secretive preparations had been for nothing. Herzl reassured him in one of his characteristic froths: "They see me walk in here alone, they think I want to do something unnatural to the seals. They see us together, they think we're just doing the usual mourning about something. Now what do you want from me, schmuck?" Back on familiar territory with the man, Gibb unfolded his peace plan: In exchange for his silence about Franchisement, Herzl could nominate a member of the board of directors for monitoring the moral content of the company's initiatives. Herzl looked disgusted with himself for feeling so amenable to the bribe, but could hardly say no when Gibb sweetened the proposal by promising to include a mention of the man's West 47th Street store "whenever some customer asks for a jewelry recommendation." After a brief attempt at demanding that Gibb list his store in all Franchisement ads, Herzl grunted and settled for appointing himself the board's moral monitor. His companions applauded the choice, then scuttled off to see the exotic birds. A week later, responding to a crack from the mayor about "those Franchisement maniacs," Herzl told his cable audience that the City Hall official "should be dragged into the street and have his blasphemous limbs pulled off."

More welcome was the reappearance of Connie Theodore. At the end of an orientation seminar for Franchisement trainees in a midtown hotel, Gibb was stunned to find his first and only serious love waiting for him. Astonishment followed astonishment. She still had the merriment in her eyes he had craved to dive into back in the university cafeteria. She had given up working at the Ford Foundation's Sociological Institute years before, using her experience there to open her own public relations firm. She had married a market research executive, divorced, married a standup comic, and divorced again. She was genuinely happy he had discovered his own piece of air to control. She wouldn't have minded having Franchisement as one of her clients. And maybe he should consider that, as soon as the novelty wore off, Franchisement might need a firm like hers to keep it before the public's attention.

Gibb was enchanted several times over. There was preamble, there was pitch, there was more preamble, there was more pitch. The personal and the commercial had never sounded so intertwined. She had finally abandoned her abstract sociological ways, all her theories, surveys, and statistics about more people than she actually was. She wanted to say only good things about people she wasn't. She seemed especially bent on saying only good things about people she wasn't. She seemed especially bent on saying only good things about him. Her eyelashes weren't quite the same black as her hair, but she still seemed to be wading at the bottom of a deep pool, waiting for him to jump in with her.

Joel Sternheim, present when Theodore accosted Gibb in the hotel lobby, recalls the scene as one of great tenderness:

> Alan and I were going to lunch to discuss the infomercial
> potential of Franchisement when Connie came walking up. The
> whole lobby, I swear, tingled. If Karl Marx had been there, he
> would've called it a synthesis of the heart.

Gibb himself described the hotel lobby encounter with Theodore "just what Franchisement and its founder needed." He told *Newsday*:

> A lot of people have a lot to say about mixing the personal
> and the financial. You look at it clearly, though, and you'll see
> that no matter what side of the debate they claim to be on,

they're usually only talking about taking an occasional break from business matters for a drink or a lay. Even at their most leisurely, in other words, most people remain in this working lunch frame of mind. But as soon as I saw Connie again, I knew that wasn't good enough. It had never been so obvious to me how much of a workaholic I'd become, how I had forgotten one of the most basic lessons of the Washington Senators Personality—if you go on neglecting quality time, you're not going to have too much quantity time, either. Any public relations needs we might have had was extra.

A review of credit card records and other circumstantial materials indicates that Gibb and Theodore went to lunch in the hotel restaurant without Joel Sternheim, then moved their reunion down to her West 23rd Street office, to a French restaurant on Hudson Street, and then to his Central Park West apartment. Over the next several weeks they dined together almost every evening, sometimes going to the theater (they attended *The Lion King* three times), sometimes to the opera (they didn't miss a moment of *Der Ring des Nibelungen* at the Westbury Music Fair), and sometimes remaining home on Central Park West or at her Chelsea place to watch videos (her taste ran to Mel Gibson and Hungarian prize winners, his to Drew Barrymore and Japanese anime). Their first trip out of the city was for a weekend stay with her sister in Providence. Although bound by a family agreement not to talk to the media, the sister, Ronnie Theodore, did reveal to one Rhode Island newsman: "They like each other. Now fuck off."

When Gibb hired Theodore as Franchisement's public relations chief, the only dissenting voice was that of the Lexington Avenue firm she displaced. Bart Patterson, for one, was impressed by the long-range plan she had blueprinted for keeping Franchisement in the public eye after it suffered some inevitable slippage as a newsworthy topic. Patterson:

I learned the hard way you can't depend on your customers always doing outrageous or important things to keep you in the papers. Even if you pitch sleaze, that's just not going to

happen. It's even more improbable when what you're selling
is GOOD NEWS. Name me a tabloid show that was all GOOD
NEWS and I'll give you a tabloid show that can't get a kinescope
into the Museum of Broadcasting. Connie made all those
worries unnecessary by coming up with a far-reaching scheme
for enlarging Franchisement's base—women and children and
immigrants, lots of those kinds of people. She saw before any of
us that if we wanted to become more universal, we had to become
more sectarian, making sure that we covered every last sectarian.

Six months after their hotel meeting, Gibb and Theodore were
wed in an open-air ceremony in Central Park before more than
3,000 witnesses. In honor of the occasion, City Hall closed down
the Sheep Meadow section of the park to all but those who wanted
to see the rites. Benjamin Acocella, who presided over the multi-
denominational service, recalls having more on the line than
formalizing the desires of the president and chief public relations
officer of Franchisement Enterprises for one another. Acocella:

The ecumenical council had been wavering on Franchisement's
membership application for a number of months. Some members
thought the business was too narrow in its rejection of the
negative, that this blinded it to the often cathartic importance
of the bad. But the turnout in the park for Alan and Connie
managed to win them over. You had pickpockets, junkies,
muggers, pushers, drunks, litterers, loiterers, the licentious, and
the lewd all over the Sheep Meadow. When the council's fence
sitters saw this, they understood that Franchisement didn't
actually ban the negative or pretend that it didn't exist, it just
wanted to skip it. I'm pleased to say Franchisement was admitted
to the council as a full-fledged mental observance a few days after
the wedding.

15

AT HOME WITH DR. ALAN GIBB AGAIN

OTH ALAN GIBB and Connie Theodore nod at the memory of their wedding ceremony in Central Park. It is as though they are both saying they remember it. "So many people," she remarks, and he nods, maybe the faintest doubt in his eyes that everybody there had actually been invited. But it is the most passing of doubts. More at hand is the prospect offered by the phone on the coffee table of taking another call. His earlier consultation with the Teutonic-sounding customer on foreign affairs has clearly whetted his appetite to be back in the trenches. He smiles happily as Connie reaches over to the receiver to instruct Duluth to pass along another caller.

In the event, the transfer takes some doing because the supervisor at the other end in Duluth had not been warned about a second intervention by the Father of Franchisement and makes two demands for Connie's credit card number before being reassured that he will always be able to find employment as an ice fishing warden if he doesn't do what he has been told. The delay has a POSITIVE side in providing enough time for Gibb to answer one of the oldest enigmas about his Journey: his early insistence, especially to a *Time* reporter, that he had 16 influential people in his life, but that, mainly because of his father, he actually had fewer mascots than that for his Personal Standings League. As one who has heard the question many times before, Gibb nods, slips a yellow Jolly Rancher into his mouth, and says:

> I guess fewer people influenced me than I had thought. Anybody who has 16 people influencing them has the personality of a sponge.

And fewer influences made for a radically less porous character? Gibb enjoys the question and gives his interlocutor the finger.

Finally, the connection is made through the Duluth office and the customer gets on the line. She sounds to be in her mid-forties, from the south, and with imitation pearls around her neck. She introduces herself as an Arizona Diamondback Personality with a Running PITS and FUNs of 361, 429, and 5,210. Gibb reminds her he isn't interested in any of that stuff until she gives him her credit card number; only with the American Express number and its expiration date on the record does he ask her what she wants.

CUSTOMER: *I've been worrying a lot lately about whether I'm really cut out to be a domestic person.*

Gibb: *A maid? You don't clean thoroughly?*

CUSTOMER: *No, no. A domestic in the sense of a home person.*

Gibb: *You want to get out of a boring marriage?*

CUSTOMER: *No, I mean whether I'm really cut out to be in the United States. Domestic, in that way. I really don't care if this place goes to hell in a handbasket. My only worry is that I just might be reading my PITS or FUN wrong or something.*

Gibb cannot disguise his surprise before the problem. Connie makes a soft click with her tongue, then notices something on her right big toe.

Gibb: *That's always possible, of course. But let's be more specific about your problem, first. You don't feel like an American, is that what you want me to understand?*

CUSTOMER: *American, un-American, I don't care about that. I'm talking about being a domestic person, the home team. When I look into a mirror that claims to be mine in my house on my block in my town in my state, I feel there's something very wrong.*

Gibb: *You feel like you don't belong.*

CUSTOMER: *Right. And that got me thinking. The old Brooklyn Dodgers used to play in New Jersey before they went to California. Does that make me a Brooklyn Dodgers Personality instead of an Arizona Diamondback Personality?*

Maybe it is only the late afternoon shadows crossing past his windows, but Alan Gibb suddenly looks frozen by the question. The woman has unknowingly dragged him back to his childhood, back to when his and Fred Gibb's Dodgers had indeed played some home games in Jersey City. It is a memory that not even seedy Australian movies about traveling salesmen has completely erased from his mind.

CUSTOMER: *You still there?*

Gibb seems to need Connie raising her right foot to her lap to snap back into the present.

GIBB: *So what you're saying is that you need an identity closer to not being a home team.*

CUSTOMER: *I was starting to think I was talking Urdu.*

GIBB: *That's a big order.*

CUSTOMER: *It's my identity. Can you deliver or can't you?*

Connie seems to have found the same substance on her right toe as she found earlier on the back of her left hand. Whatever it is, one of its cardinal properties appears to be invisibility.

GIBB: *If that's what you want, no problem.*

CUSTOMER: *Yes, that's what I want.*

GIBB: *Okay, for the sake of argument, let's put you down as a Brooklyn Dodgers Personality.*

CUSTOMER: You *argue. That's what I want.*

GIBB: *Brooklyn Dodgers it is, then. And I'd recommend keeping your Running PITS.*

CUSTOMER: *That's alright with me. I never had any problem with my PITS. Least that I know about.*

GIBB: *Then I'm sure you haven't. Which gets us now to your FUNs. Do you have any new preferences in that area?*

CUSTOMER: *I'm open to suggestions. What do you think?*

Gibb is diverted by Connie's examination of her toe. He seems a little uncomfortable to have her with her foot in front of her face with outsiders in the room. He waves for her to lower her leg. She ignores him. He throws the six or seven Jolly Rancher wrappings in his hand at her, but he has failed to ball them adequately, and they barely get beyond his knee before they begin floating to the coffee table and the floor. But at least Connie catches the movement from the papers, and she looks up into Gibb's scowl. The meter in her eyes makes several clicks before she understands his pantomiming. She gives off an embarrassed little smile and returns her foot to the carpet.

CUSTOMER: *What're you doing? Killing time on the clock?*

GIBB: *No, Ma'am. What I was trying to work out here was a FUN for you that would be entirely positive and joyous and would simultaneously let you feel like the foreigner you are.*

CUSTOMER: *I didn't say I felt like a foreigner. I just said I didn't feel like the real me was on the domestic side of things. That the only alternative—you got to feel like a foreigner?*

Gibb ponders the question. He gives the impression of never having considered it before at any great length.

CUSTOMER: *You there?*

GIBB: *Well, yes, I suppose there's the other alternative of just feeling like you're away all the time.*

CUSTOMER: *"Away?"*

Connie jabs her index finger at Gibb in a ringing endorsement of what he has proposed to the customer. He seems almost giddily happy with his unexpected discovery.

GIBB: *Away. You find your JOY and FREEDOM in visiting. You can be an American, a Portuguese, or a Malaysian. It doesn't matter what you are, it's where you are. And where you are is always on a visit. You're the ultimate Away team.*

There is a pregnant silence on the console speaker. It becomes almost possible to see the customer fingering the pearls around her neck as she mulls over what Gibb has said to her. She pulls the pearls left and then right and then left again. Maybe a blue jay flies past the window she is gazing through from her telephone as she reflects and pulls. Finally comes a whisper.

CUSTOMER: *I see what you're saying.*

Gibb mimes a "Whew!" on Fifth Avenue.

CUSTOMER: *A non-domestic issue doesn't have to be a foreign issue. It can be a domestic issue, too.*

GIBB: *That's correct. You just have to keep on the move.*

CUSTOMER: *Then what are you saying about my FUNs?*

Gibb is back on solid ground, dealing cards as dexterously as a poker sharpie. He even stands up to retrieve another tube of Jolly Ranchers from a sideboard. His voice carries confidently over to the speaker as he rips a gash at one end of the sweets.

GIBB: *1,956 is one possibility. That's when the interstate highway act was passed in Congress.*

CUSTOMER: *Sounds good.*

GIBB: *Now, now, don't just say that because I suggested it. Pick a FUN you are comfortable with. You're the one who's going to have to live with it after you hang up.*

CUSTOMER: *I appreciate that.*

GIBB: *Then take your time. There are other possibilities. You've got 66, for example.*

CUSTOMER: *That sounds awfully close to devil worship. No, I'll be fine with that 1,956.*

GIBB: *Just that one? There's no extra charge for a second or third one, you know.*

CUSTOMER: *That one is fine. Thank you very much.*

The customer hangs up before Gibb can even tell her what Famous Franchisement Folks she now shares readings with. He lets the meter run another minute anyway, if only to get back at her rudeness. Connie excuses herself with some awkward hopping out of the living room; whatever she has found on her toe, she is clearly determined to keep it there until she gets to the bathroom for a closer inspection.

Gibb reclaims his chair near the window and watches after Connie a moment. Then his eyes drop to the console on the coffee table. The customer hadn't been all that wrong, perhaps: There *is* the look of the devil in the Father of Franchisement.

"Why don't we try one more?" he says conspiratorially, already reaching down to punch one of the buttons by himself.

16

THE FIRST COUPLE

ASIDE FROM STRIKING another mother lode of publicity for his venture as a whole, Gibb's Central Park wedding brought attention to the first woman of significance directly involved in Franchisement. Jennifer Pryor, for one, believes this has consolidated Franchisement's institutional appeal. Harvard's Dean of Theoretical Business observes:

> However sincere he was about making a charting sensitive to
> multi-gendered priorities, Alan had remained hobbled by the fact
> that he wasn't a multi-gendered personally. It's like somebody
> with one eye saying he understands the advantages of being
> 20/20 in both eyes: Until he gets his second eye straightened out,
> he's just a lot of empty words. Connie contributed a credibility
> that made it easier for women everywhere to take out their cell
> phones and get in touch with a Franchisement counselor.

Statistics bear out Pryor. In its first two years, Franchisement Enterprises received 79 percent of its calls from men, males, or voices claiming to belong to a similar category; in the wake of Gibb's marriage to Theodore, women rose to account for 53 percent of the callers. And, as Pryor has noted, 67 percent of those women have been under 21:

> Women in their teens or barely out of them are especially hungry for positive self-images. If you exclude Sappho, Joan of Arc, and Buffy the Vampire Slayer, though, you'll see western history has supplied them with very few models for positive reinforcement. In turning to Connie and Alan, they are essentially asking for what centuries of Judaic-Christian culture has failed to give them.

In recent years, children have also become more conspicuous among ratepayers, doubling their presence from 8 to 16 percent. Key initiatives for achieving this have included buying commercial TV time during critical Saturday morning cartoon hours and entering into supply agreements with elementary schools in 43 states. Sidney Willinger points to the latter as having been particularly fruitful in attracting minors. Willinger:

> The computer companies got along for years selling schools on the idea that sitting before a keyboard was a leisure activity. Right. And so is going into the mountains with your boss and office rivals for a week of survivor sports. By giving schools cell phones that both kids and teachers could use right at their desks or even take home with them, Alan restored fun to activity hours. And thanks to Bart Patterson, overhead costs were minimal.

Franchisement's steady growth helped make Gibb and Theodore "personalities" in ways not covered by their own company concept. Rarely did a week go by that they weren't photographed at some charity or social event. *Architecture Digest* and other let-them-eat-cake periodicals did opulent spreads on their penthouse apartment. Their mere presence at a Rangers game in Madison Square Garden in March 2000 sparked rumors that Franchisement Enterprises was about to use hockey franchises as a new psychognomical tool. When Alan hosted "Saturday Night Live" a month later, his willingness to take a joke at his own expense added further warmth to his image, reminding the nation of the effervescent personality who had delighted talk show hosts in promoting *I'm a Peewee, You're a Bambino.* Connie became such a visible spokesperson for the company that she was routinely consulted on overnight cable shows in any crisis having a mental factor—school shootings, FBI sieges, Congressional elections, etc. But the most marked sign of the First Couple's new status came in the invitation they received in February 2000 to join other White House guests at an official dinner for the visiting prime minister of Sri Lanka. The invitation was significant not only because they were asked to break bread with the President of the United States, but because their presence had been explicitly requested by the prime minister, Ranasinghe Bandaranaike (who, after a midnight consultation in his hotel suite, agreed he was a Los Angeles Dodger Personality with a Raincheck PITS and FUNs of 18, 321, and 489.) As Joel Sternheim has said:

> Bandaranaike's request made Franchisement an international phenomenon. As soon as he declared he was this one thing, it was easier for the Tamils and Sinhalese to sit down and know where the other guy was coming from. I think the armistice in their civil war there is fully to Alan's credit, and we can only hope that when Bandaranaike asks for a new reading, he'll continue to think a ceasefire in Sri Lanka is compatible with his personality.

Not that there haven't been some rough patches in the personal and professional lives of the First Couple, of course. But most of these have been private, nobody's business but their own. Bart Patterson:

> You like to know what shape your partners are in because you never know when some frying pan scene in the kitchen will depress your investment. But sometimes they listened through me when I called to ask how they were. They just didn't want me to know how they were.

Sidney Willinger, Jennifer Pryor, and Joel Sternheim have reported similar cold shoulders on occasion. "I've been stymied more than once by what's been going on with them," Willinger can admit. "Have they been in an argument about something to do with Franchisement or just because he left the toilet seat up again? That doubt is always one of the down sides about mixing the personal with the leisurely."

Jennifer Pryor also concedes that she has sometimes been reduced to speculating on the nature of the trouble in the Fifth Avenue penthouse. "When a couple refuses to talk about a marriage that others have a stake in," she points out, "you can be pretty sure he's been a shit in some way and she's decided to play the martyr. It's no coincidence that more than 44 percent of the martyrs in Christian mythology have been women."

While not as definitive as it could be, evidence suggests that Gibb and Theodore weathered their heaviest storm as a couple in the fall of 2004, following a public attack on the Father of Franchisement by Gloria Tavarez. The ugliness started when Tavarez, a psychiatrist with an 18-year practice in Pittsburgh, requested her file from the FBI in 2000 under the Freedom of Information Act. When she finally received it four years later, she was dismayed to discover she had been under what was termed "loose surveillance" most of her life since moving from San Juan to the mainland. Almost as astonishing, she learned from the mounds of heavily censored onionskins sent to her, the surveillance had been instituted after an unnamed "high school classmate approached an agent during a tour of FBI headquarters in Washington . . . expressing misgivings about the subject's legal status in the United States." The timing of the information proved fateful insofar as Tavarez, fresh off the World Series win by the Red Sox, no longer felt like a born loser. Moreover, the quasi-revelations from the FBI file coincided with a Franchisement campaign to draw more immigrants to the telephone. As Tavarez told *Newsweek*:

> Sure, I'd thought of Gibb as this anonymous informer. But I didn't really convince myself of it until I saw this ad on TV one night. It turned my stomach. It was like those ads the tobacco companies flood the ghettos with, appealing to the street-smart macho. "Hey, Esteban, you really sure you like loving them and leaving them as an Atlanta Braves Personality?" "What about it,

Chou—wondering why those Cincinnati Reds losers without your science degrees still end up with all the best lab jobs?" Suddenly, I couldn't think of anybody *but* Gibb.

With the help of one-time classmate Richie Burke, principal of her old high school, Tavarez took the precaution of tracking down the other students recorded as having taken the trip to Washington. Only with them eliminated as suspects did she call Gibb.

He did a lot of stuttering, saying he couldn't remember that far back. Then he got mad I'd ever think such a thing about him. We shared "too much," he kept saying. All I remembered is that we made out in the alleyway next to my house a couple of times. As if that made us Romeo and Juliet!

Three weeks after their telephone conversation, Tavarez aired her charges for the first time, during a Scranton conference on "The Paranormal Paranoid Personality: Psychoses Emanating from Non-Human Agents." When a local newspaper reported her remarks, the doctor was thrust into the limelight. Not even her prudence about wording her allegations and the refusal of the FBI to confirm them deterred the media from trying to use her as a battering ram into the most private sanctums of Franchisement and its First Couple. Instead of issuing daily releases on the latest success story inspired by a charting, Theodore found herself having to repeat over and over again how she couldn't have cared less about her husband's adventures in puppy love and how Gloria Tavarez's problems with federal authorities had nothing to do with Franchisement's immigrant campaign since Puerto Ricans were Americans, not immigrants. For his part, Gibb wondered whether some Pittsburgh residents hadn't allowed envy to cloud their reason, reassuring them that the exclusion of the Pirates from the Personal Standings League didn't mean they had to regard themselves as outsiders.

But these responses did little to stop the waters from boiling over in one East Side penthouse—or from engulfing an old friend. Linda McElligott:

I hadn't heard from Alan for some time, so I was taken off guard when he suddenly called one night, saying he needed to hear a friendly voice. I took that to mean the *esposa* was on his case for something. Of course, Alan being Alan, he also wanted more than my voice.

In fact, Gibb asked McElligott to arrange a meeting for him with a delegation of representatives from Central and South American immigrants in New York. The commissive language expert admits to admiring his gall:

> Here's a man's who's never even eaten a taco and he's asking me to organize some happening that'll make him look like an old friend of Latin America! Politicians up for an election couldn't be smarmier!
>
> *So why did she agree to set up the meeting?* As long as I'd known Alan, I'd always been on him to commit to the path he had set out upon. He wanted to be smarmy? I could hardly tell him not to be so committed to it.

Thanks to McElligott's Rolodex, Gibb met in a Washington Heights auditorium with a group that included two members of the city council, three assemblymen, the vice-president of the Better Business Bureau, the regional director of the Immigration and Naturalization Service, and a *Daily News* columnist who hadn't written about anything but Gloria Tavarez's accusations for weeks. The highly publicized encounter turned out to be only the first of many involving the city's immigrant population, and set the POSITIVE tone that would characterize subsequent sessions with Chinese, Korean, Vietnamese, Indian, Pakistani, Russian, Ukrainian, Greek, Turkish, Sudanese, Saudi, Danish, Belgian, Maltese, and Irish community leaders. (An Italian group boycotted a scheduled get-together when it learned that neither Enrico Fermi nor Sophia Loren was listed as one of Franchisement's Famous Folks.) The tenor of the meetings was described by Theodore Herzl, who brought Gibb together with a delegation from Crown Heights. Herzl:

I told the *schnook* before he went in—you got to be aggressive.
The only reason these people aren't classified as refugees is
nobody from the Red Cross asked them to lay down in a big field.
Otherwise, they're the bread crumbs of God. They fly into an
airport here and they see women walking around naked even in
January. All these *shmendriks* are lost, I reminded him. They're
looking for a little positive guidance, and if it's between you and
that brown *shiksa* in Pittsburgh, they'll even take it from you.

Accounts of Gibb's demeanor at the succession of meetings
agree that he exuded the self-confidence counseled by Herzl. For
Linda McElligott, he was "committed to being manipulative, fully
so." For Vlasta Sorenko, head of the Brighton Beach Neighborhood
Club, he "didn't make the mistake of a half-man by apologizing for
everything." For Brendan O'Grady of Irish Citizenship Initiatives,
he "gave you the guff you expected to hear, but as long as you knew
he knew you knew it was all guff, there was no reason not to get on
with it."

Public comments of the kind effectively drowned out the attacks
from Tavarez and anti-Franchisement thrill seekers. Moreover,
after the crisis had peaked, Theodore was able to issue a release
announcing more than 4,000 additional customers, only 14 of
whom had English as a first language. "They view Franchisement
as just another enhancement of their right to the American Dream,"
the release asserted.

Whatever tensions had existed in the Gibb-Theodore household
were also dissipated by the meetings with the community leaders.
After an absence of some weeks from the society pages of the *Times*,
the First Couple again began being photographed with regularity
at openings, premieres, and fund-raising events for the New York
Public Library. And while Theodore professed gratitude that, as she
told one columnist, "so many people should be concerned about
the flu Alan and I had," Gibb was slightly more forthcoming with
Linda McElligott during the cocktail party launching her follow up
to *Omissive Language, Commissive Language—It's All Language,
Salsa—It's All Language.* McElligott:

As usual, when he didn't want anything from me, I had to pull teeth. Had he been through a rough time with the *esposa*? He nodded. A rough time triggered by the Tavarez business? He nodded. Had they slept together during the big chill? Shake of the head. Had they wandered off in search of other companions? None of my business. Had it been exciting for both of them? A nod and a shrug. Had he and Theodore buried the hatchet? He finally smiled. "I'm in control of my air again," he said. To me, that said the *matrimonio* was back on track.

And remains so. If there has been any change in the lives of Alan Gibb and Connie Theodore over recent times, it has been in their almost evangelical determination to share their success with Franchisement with the less fortunate. They have contributed generously (and anonymously) to the United States Congress, the Jerry Lewis Telethon, and numerous monthly magazines. They have purchased foster children in Chile and Sweden, maintaining regular correspondences (and free chartings) with their charges. They have underwritten scholarships for Franchisement studies in numerous institutions of higher learning, including Harvard's School for Theoretical Business, the University of Indiana's Leisure Sciences Department, and the Brooklyn Yeshiva of Blut und Eisen. Perhaps just as impressive, they have made it policy never to contest the rare reasonable complaint from a dissatisfied customer, and for this alone they have been cited for meritorious service by numerous consumer groups. As the plaque they received in February 2000 from Better Business Bureau *jefe* Manuel Vargas declared: "Franchisement is a business that doesn't give its customers the business."

All of this has left long-time acquaintances, even the initially skeptical and contemptuous, convinced of the HEALTHY RELATIONSHIP that exists between Gibb and Franchisement. Linda McElligott:

There's no question Alan has gotten as much out of Franchisement as it's gotten out of him. He has beliefs in himself and he's not afraid to believe in them.

Father Benjamin Acocella concurs:

After all his spiritual, physical, and economic roamings, Alan is finally at peace with himself. The Wandering in the Desert is over. The Long March is over. The New York Marathon is over.

17

WHERE'S WHO

WHILE GIBB AND Theodore have been the most conspicuous beneficiaries of Franchisement's success, they have hardly been the only ones. Most important of all have been the millions of customers around the world who have secured a greater sense of identity through Franchisement counseling. If they have not all been able to exploit their FUNs and PITS for instant financial gain, or even been able to point to Personal Standings League compatibilities to account for happy marriages, bright children, or pleasant vacations, they have almost to a customer been able to say they gained a sense of direction faster than they would have by consulting some storefront fortune teller. As Joel Sternheim has observed: "You can say all you want about Alan's genius, Connie's flair for getting media attention, or Bart Patterson's money, but if you don't have customers, you don't have anything. Hegel hinted at it, Marx formulated it, and Gibb has made it real."

Sternheim himself hasn't done too badly by Franchisement. An assistant sound engineer for a pro-Castro pirate radio station in the Miami area when he first heard of Alan Gibb, he turned his back on that career to become assistant office manager for the

900-FRANCHLY operation in Orlando. Within a couple of years, Sternheim, up to that point a mixture of anarchism and Fabianism in his social outlook, had displayed enough mastery of corporate organization to be offered an assistant professorship at the Miami State University Business School. Now among the school's most recognized faculty members, he has set up his own video company with the backing of Franchisement Enterprises and plans to control a percentage of any franchising spin-offs the economy makes necessary in the future. He confides a hope the economy will never make that necessary.

Theodore Herzl has profited from his association with Franchisement to the point of being regarded as a viable candidate in New York City's next mayoralty elections. Although he has yet to issue a formal threat to enter the race, he has been devoting more of his cable shows since the turn of the millennium to non-Hasid lobby groups that would be crucial to him in such a run. Superficially, the shows have followed the course of the programs ever since they have been on the air—an opening question about the guest's attitude toward the secular leaders of Israel, a tirade against the guest's mealy-mouthed reply, and the damning of the guest's bloodline. But with the likes of William Donovan of the Catholic Morality for All League, Jamal Smith of the Ancient Order of Liberians, and Costas Papandropolos of the Turkey Belongs to Greece Defense Fund, Herzl has also provided a forum for the dignitaries to join in denunciations of his pet peeves and to salute him for his efforts as the Franchisement board's morality monitor. Typical of his success was a coordinated April 2001 attack by Donovan, Smith, and Francis Singh of the Ethnic Newspaper Guild on City Hall for spurning Herzl's demand that all Crown Heights street signs be converted to Hebrew. Most local observers viewed it as a victory for the emerging coalition when city authorities agreed to the compromise of allowing a second, Hebrew sign to be posted under the existing English one. Even the normally hard-to-please Herzl had to admit the compromise made it "hard even for my *shmuck* of a brother-in-law to get lost."

Bart Patterson has seen his investment in Franchisement multiply and multiply again, consolidating his reputation in the world of high finance. If there has been any downside to his success, it has been in the appearance of Gail and Leslie Daly, one-time users of his 666 line who have charged that Patterson's financial gains were proof that, as the sisters told the Jesuit weekly *America*, "the Master has been among us all along." The Dalys said they were "unconcerned, even flattered" that Patterson swore out a restraining order against them, promising "we will be here when we are needed for the Final Conflict."

Even before her School for Theoretical Business benefited from the Franchisement fellowship program, Harvard's Jennifer Pryor had reason to be grateful to Gibb. In the three years leading up to the endowment, in fact, an ever-increasing percentage of Harvard freshmen had cited Franchisement as the reason for their decision to transfer to her specialization. As Pryor has explained it:

> There's a common misconception theoretical business is all abstraction, the antithesis to a business business. Nothing could be further from the truth. Within the abstractions of the theoretical business, it is still imperative to have concrete abstractions, the business business. Otherwise, you're just swimming in a drained pool. Franchisement's concrete abstractness appealed a great deal to the next generation, enabling us at the school to do a great deal of business—both kinds.

Like Pryor, Sidney Willinger has seen enrolments rise dramatically in his Leisure Sciences department since Franchisement gained a grip on the national consciousness. The growth has been so marked since 1996 that the department entered the new millennium claiming more undergraduates than the Sports History department, Indiana University's chief recruitment draw for more than 30 years. Over the same period, the university's publishing arm has issued 25 Masters theses and six doctorates with Franchisement themes. Willinger himself has penned a study of Franchisement entitled *When Winning Teams Are the Only Teams—Franchisement in Mass Culture*. Lacking authorization from Gibb to reveal any of the background on Franchisement's development, indeed even under the threat of a lawsuit if he did so, Willinger confined himself to referring to the phenomenon within an historical context that he then rehashed from his own writings on such subjects as Marshall McLuhan, Tex Ritter westerns, and Dungeons and Dragons. Impressed by Willinger's willingness to take no for an answer, Gibb invited him to join the company board.

Not everybody has been given such an opportunity. When Archie Geis called from Santa Fe with a proposal that every psychognomy in the Personal Standings League be assigned a GM auto model, Gibb asked how his mother was. He would have been better off not asking because, as soon as she got on the phone, Louise told him she and Jesus were both entitled to seats on the board, automatically giving her two votes. Ever since that phone conversation, Gibb admits, he has confined his contacts with New Mexico to whatever the tape on his message machine picks up. There is little doubt he grieves quietly and privately over his all but severed ties with his mother and stepfather, but since he does so quietly and privately, he never shows it.

As for Randy Rolf, her role in launching *You're a Peewee, I'm a Bambino* has made her a ubiquitous presence in publishing circles. When she hasn't been chairing panels for discussing such topics as the decline of the e-novel, she has been acquiring best sellers like *Thomas Edison's Most Idiotic Inventions* and *Why Little Men Always Want to Do Big Things*. She has also found time for her own writing, most prominently with *Randy Rolf: Unedited* and its sequel *Randy Rolf: With Footnotes*. Although she has claimed on more than one occasion that she doesn't feel any debt to Alan Gibb or to Franchisement for her career rise, that she would have found equal fulfillment from any other manuscript in her slush pile, some insiders have described her as resentful that Gibb has not only declined to write a follow-up to *You're a Peewee, I'm a Bambino*, but also to put up the seed money for a projected monthly magazine entitled *Randy*.

Father Benjamin Acocella, for one, says such resentment, real or imagined, doesn't surprise him. Acocella:

> Despite my own efforts, you can't please all the people all the time. Randy's attitude is a proof in the pudding and the pilaf.

But I can also recommend we take a POSITIVE from that—that in her very attitude toward Alan, Randy is illustrating the truth of what some might think is only a worthless bromide. She is showing us the bromide isn't the least bit worthless, that there will indeed always be a person or two displeased by what is going on around them. And I believe that redounds in the last analysis to the credit of Alan and the GOOD he has always sought to introduce us to through Franchisement. If we can reaffirm even what appears to be stale, trite, and evasive, what horizons remain beyond the reach of the human frolic?

18

WHAT'S WHAT

ANY EVALUATION OF Franchisement's significance in the modern world must begin with the French philosopher Francois La Rochefoucauld's (approximately translated) observation that "every revolution gains its validity merely in the greater freedom won for a single individual one as a result of." Although unfashionable since he stated it in the 17th century, La Rochefoucauld's viewpoint represents a plausible response to the age-old challenge of having social action accommodate both the unique and the mass, the specific something and the everything else. And by that criterion Franchisement has not only passed the test, it has aced it. Testimonials of "greater freedom" achieved through the Franchisement process—a few of them even unsolicited—have numbered in the countless. Little wonder that the ecumenicist Benjamin Acocella has been moved to remark that "if the Russian Revolution had prompted similar expressions of gratitude for liberation, the Berlin Wall not only wouldn't have been knocked down, it would have been emulated by nations around the globe."

La Rochefoucauld made a second observation relevant to the growth of Franchisement. As related in his noted *Memories*, dealing with the 17th-century taxation uprising against the French crown, he encountered "many a rebel whose countenance of purposefulness and action of zeal terrorized by their very dedication," inspiring him to ask: "When man wants something so badly, can there be any good inside it?" There would seem to be little doubt that, for the "action of zeal" known as Franchisement, Alan Gibb has answered the question resoundingly in the affirmative. On a personal level, he has avoided the traditional trap of permitting his success to detour him into megalomania and obsessive self-enrichment; to this day, and despite constant exposure to the media and the man on the street, his hungers remain subdued to the rim of impassivity. On a business level, he has endorsed the dominance of information as the most precious modern commodity while also extending this priority to a 24-hour-a-day empathy with every individual in possession of a telephone and credit card, no matter what their payment plans.

And then there is this: Through his insight, energy, and corporate structure, Alan Gibb has empowered countless masses who, rather than resort to the often-tawdry sublimations of addictive drugs, laugh-track sitcoms, and spectator sports (yes, major league baseball included), spend their time grasping for a sense of identity they can be comfortable with. Evidently in success, but equally in their (instantly reversible) failures, these customers have come to function with unprecedented vibrancy in the workplace, in the family hearth, and in the supermarket parking lot. Like Alan Gibb himself, every one of them can say that the society in which he was born is not the society in which he is creeping toward death. One and all, they have overcome their feeling of disenfranchisement.

And the future?

The venerable ideator seems puzzled by the question for a moment. But it turns out he is merely bewildered that the last two Jolly Ranchers in his tube are both green. He opines that somebody along the factory conveyor belt "must have fucked up."

And the future? The prospects for Franchisement Enterprises and the society that has come to rely on it for so much?

There is a shriek from the next room before Gibb can reply. He looks toward the door apprehensively but not anxiously. Connie has apparently found another invisible imperfection somewhere. Since she is bothered where she is, the male half of the First Couple is equally bothered for her. But when there is no subsequent shriek, he goes back to muttering about the Jolly Rancher foreman who wasn't vigilant against two green candies being stacked together.

Once again the question about the future, and this time Gibb offers enough attention to shrug. "You gotta take it one day at a time," he says.

A modesty ingrained from his brutal experiences during The Journey? We'll let that one go unanswered for now.

GLOSSARY

Follows a list of Franchisement's most commonly used terms and acronyms. Standard dictionaries and encyclopedias should provide fuller definitions for many of the terms.

Baseball – The sport of debatably American origin whose team structure suggested an organizational structure for Franchisement. It is played in the United States, Canada, Japan, Taiwan, South Korea, Australia, vast areas of Latin America, and scattered pockets of Europe.

Counselors – The living guides to Franchisement enlightenment, stationed in Enid, Oklahoma and Duluth, Minnesota.

Credit Cards – Plastic conveniences distributed by financial firms for facilitating payment for the enlightenment provided by Franchisement counselors. Unlike cash, they guarantee written reports of transactions and have fixed serial numbers.

Customers – Franchisement's primary interlocutors, encompassing all sexes, ages, social inclinations, ethnic groups, nationalities, income levels, credit cards, and area codes.

FFF – The acronym for Famous Franchisement Folks—personages from any time dimension who have been strongly identified with specific franchise typologies.

FUN – The acronym for Franchisement's Unique Numbers—the digits, integers, and figures that denominate the numerical factors of character.

Journey, The – The popular term for Alan Gibb's odyssey through the travails that guided him toward his Franchisement vision.

Location – The decision tool adopted by Customers for identifying their personal entries into the Franchisement process.

Omissive Language – Alan Gibb's specialization before acquiring his Franchisement vision and influential for many of its precepts; now largely untaught.

Personal Standings League – The array of typologies available to Customers for their free and joyous selection.

PITS – The acronym for Positional Identity Trait Sign—a critical key for particularizing characterologies and complicating the Franchisement system. The five signs are Hitting, Pitching, Fielding, Running, and Rainchecks.

Self – The object of desire for the typical Franchisement supplicant. It can usually be located (*see Location entry)* within a customer's personality through a rigorous question-and-answer process with Counselors for varying lengths of time.

Sixteen – The FUN (see separate entry) most likely to bestow FREEDOM, PROFIT, and JOY.

Telephone – The generic name for the communication tool favored by 100 percent of Franchisement's Customers for engaging in dialogue with company Counselors.

You're a Peewee, I'm a Bambino – The best seller, translated into 36 languages (including Braille and signing), that projected the Franchisement vision into every American neighborhood and foreign enclave. (Sometimes rumored to be followed eventually by the sequel *Or Maybe You Prefer Being a Bambino, too?* —gossip repeatedly denied by Alan Gibb.)

Zero – The FUN most likely to prompt Customers to switch to the FUN Sixteen.

FRANCHISEMENT PERSONALITY CHART

What follows is the Franchisement Personality Chart employed by company counselors as the starting point in their dealings with customers. All primary qualities, of course, are subject to the influences of conjoining PITS attributes and functions (described at the end of the chart), so that all typologies ultimately ratify the GOOD sought by customers.

(While providing a comprehensive picture of the identity options available to customers, the Franchisement Personality Chart can never serve as a substitute for the dynamics of one-on-one communication with 900-FRANCHLY counselors. Consequently, readers are warned not to anticipate that private pleasure with the chart will yield definitive insights into their selves, souls, or spirits. Practical results from such leisure activities cannot be guaranteed, and any lawsuits, public criticisms, or libels of Franchisement Enterprises, its employees, sponsors, or well-wishers stemming from unfounded expectations or mental-emotional disillusionments will be rebutted to the most strenuous legal and financial degree.)

BROOKLYN DODGERS

The Brooklyn Dodger Personality is rooted in swagger, heartache, and repressed bitterness. Its principal discordants are the New York Giants, New York Yankees, and Los Angeles Dodgers. Its main concordant is the New York Mets. Its favorite stone is an opal (on sale at Herzl and Son, 49 West 47th Street, New York, New York 10036). FUN—1, 4, 6, 14, 39, 42.

FFF—Nero, St. Teresa of Avila, Saladin, John Quincy Adams, Clara Barton, Cher, and Fred Gibb.

NEW YORK GIANTS

The New York Giants Personality exudes dissipation, dissembling, and parasitism. Its principal discordants are the Brooklyn Dodgers, New York Yankees, and San Francisco Giants. Its main concordant is the Arizona Diamondbacks. Its favorite beverage is produced by Williamsburg Breweries.

FUN—0, 2, 19, 23, 24, 7,876.

FFF—Robert the Bruce, Paul Revere, Fernando Botero, Jackie Gleason, Mickey Rourke, and Louise Gibb.

NEW YORK YANKEES

The New York Yankees Personality is imperious, ruthless, and criminal. Its principal discordants are all other franchises. It has no concordants. Its favorite institution of higher learning is the Harvard School of Theoretical Business.

FUN—all single- and two-digit numbers.

FFF—The Golem of Prague, John Calvin, Bram Stoker, Dame Myra Hess, Joey Adams, and Archie Geis.

PHILADELPHIA PHILLIES

The Philadelphia Phillies Personality is deceptive, dolorous, and abusive. It claims to have no discordants and to love all other franchises as concordants. Its favorite branch of medicine is dentistry.

FUN—All fractions higher than 2/3.

FFF—Aristarchus of Samos, Richard the Lion Heart, Thomas Paine, G.K. Chesterton, Lili St. Cyr, and Teddy Doofle.

BOSTON RED SOX

The Boston Red Sox Personality is colorless, resigned, and envious. Its principal discordants are the New York Yankees and New York Mets. Its main concordant is the Chicago Cubs. Its favorite name is O'Reilly.

FUN—8, 9, 1919, 1920, 1946, 1978, 1986.

FFF—Pythagoras, Leif Ericson, William Tell, Maria Montessori, Babe Ruth, Arthur Schlesinger, Jr., and Gloria Tavarez.

WASHINGTON SENATORS

The Washington Senators Personality is mythical, traitorous, and misanthropic. Its principal discordants depend on opportunities of the moment, as do its main concordants. Its favorite government agency is the Federal Bureau of Investigation.

FUN. All numbers after one trillion.

FFF. Solon, John the Baptist, Pope Joan, Sara Bernhardt, Mary Eddy Baker, Walter Mondale, and Alan Gibb.

NEW YORK METS

The New York Mets Personality is delusional, recidivist, and schizophrenic. Its principal discordants are the New York Yankees, Atlanta Braves, and Los Angeles Dodgers. Its main concordants are the Brooklyn Dodgers and New York Giants. Its favorite mode of travel is out-of-body experiences.

FUN—14, 17, 31, 37, 41.

FFF—Pope Leo X, John Paul Jones, Salmon P. Chase, Harry Houdini, Dinah Shore, and Bart Patterson.

ATLANTA BRAVES

The Atlanta Braves Personality is faithless, monopolistic, and capricious. Its principal discordant is the New York Mets. Its main concordant is any personality it can merge with for greater attention to itself. Its favorite non-profit front is the Ecumenical Council on Mental Observances (President: Benjamin Acocella, S.J.).

FUN—8, 17, and any other one.

FFF—Alexander the Great, St. Francis of Assisi, George Sand, Pablo Picasso, Phyllis Diller, and Connie Theodore.

CLEVELAND INDIANS

The Cleveland Indians Personality is stereotypical, bombastic, and uncouth. Its principal discordant is the New York Yankees. Its main concordant is the Atlanta Braves. Its favorite songs require drums.

FUN—Open to suggestions.

FFF—Johann Gutenberg, Rose of Trawley, William Penn, Betsy Ross, D.W. Griffith, J. Edgar Hoover, and Theodore Herzl.

CINCINNATI REDS

The Cincinnati Reds Personality is paranoid, intolerant, and cheap. Its principal discordant is a figment of its imagination. Its main concordant is unimaginable. Its favorite food is anything from a can.
FUN—5, 14, 57, 902.
FFF—Minerva, Augustine, John Donne, Marie Antoinette, Sitting Bull, Balto, Senator Joseph McCarthy, and Lenore Kindall.

ST. LOUIS CARDINALS

The St. Louis Cardinals Personality is irresponsible, manipulative, and hazardous to health. Its principal discordant is the Chicago Cubs. Its main concordant is tomorrow's. Its favorite TV show is infomercials. (For further information, contact Joel Sternheim, Miami State University Business School, Miami, Florida.)
FUN—6, 9, 20, 104, 541.
FFF—William Shakespeare, Clara Schumann, John Pershing, Bess Truman, Rita Coolidge, and Matthew Pine.

CHICAGO CUBS

The Chicago Cubs Personality is warped, slavish, and fatalistic. Its principal discordant is the St. Louis Cardinals. Its main concordant is the Boston Red Sox. Its favorite technological development is virtual reality.
FUN—0, 14, 20, 666.
FFF—Cleopatra, Socrates, Vincent Van Gogh, Faisal I, Gig Young, and Casey Williams.

HOUSTON ASTROS

The Houston Astros Personality is exploitative, without historical memory, and unintelligible. Its principal discordants and concordants have been lost to the record. Its favorite leisure activity is guessing.
FUN—0 and any number after it.
FFF—The Unknown Soldier and Audrey Teller.

ARIZONA DIAMONDBACKS

The Arizona Diamondbacks Personality is whorish, jealous, and randy. Its principal discordant is any personality seeking a concordant relationship. Its favorite elevator group is the Hugo Winterhalter orchestra.

FUN—33, 45, 51.

FFF—Empress Theodora, John Keats, Wyatt Earp, Claudette Colbert, Indira Gandhi, and Linda McElligott.

SAN FRANCISCO GIANTS

The San Francisco Giants Personality is slow, windy, and vindictive. Its principal discordants are the New York Giants and Los Angeles Dodgers. It wouldn't recognize a concordant. Its favorite science is leisure activities (for further information, contact Dr. Sidney Willinger, Leisure Science Department, University of Indiana, Bloomington, Indiana).

FUN—Any number that evens the score.

FFF—Icarus, Johann Sebastian Bach, Ethel Barrymore, Chou En-Lai, Ella Fitzgerald, and Walter Luderus.

LOS ANGELES DODGERS

The Los Angeles Dodgers Personality is shallow, cretinous, and corrupt. Its principal discordants are the New York Mets, San Francisco Giants, and Brooklyn Dodgers. It hasn't a prayer of ever finding a concordant. Its favorite charity is one that shows an annual profit.

FUN—0, 00, 000, 0000.

FFF—The Virgin Mother, Walter Raleigh, Nat Turner, Amelia Earhart, Milton Berle, and Abner Adams.

PITS

From the starting points above, readers must next LOCATE the PITS layering their franchise choice. The PITS, it will be recalled, offer the following adaptations:

1. HITTING. Aggressive, usually self-absorbed, but capable of sacrifices; humorless; not especially bright; neurotic; ill-tempered.

2. PITCHING. Aggressive; committed to group success over individual achievement, but only if playing the dominating role in attaining that objective; intelligent; glib; slow to anger but hard to appease; self-satisfied.

3. FIELDING. Defensive; guilt-laden; tries to be ingratiating; capable of sterling accomplishments; intelligent about his job but not much else; antic humor; eager for physical confrontation.

4. RUNNING. Irresponsible; often stupid; adventurous; health conscious; indifferent to others; greedy; slick.

5. RAINCHECK. Procrastinating; evasive; arbitrary; susceptible to boredom; banks on ulterior purposes.

It is important to remember that even when both a Personal Standings typology and the applied PITS appear negative, they interact much like two negative numbers, producing a POSITIVE number. Consequently, there is never any danger of a reading that depresses or otherwise discomfits a customer. Applied to the New York Giants Personality, for example, the PITS opens up such positive possibilities as:

Hitting: Aggressiveness makes dissipation eclectic; neuroses excuse dissembling; the openness to sacrifice emboldens parasitism.

Pitching: Glibness makes dissipation amusing; intelligence assures creative dissembling; commitment to group success justifies parasitism.

Fielding: Dissipation becomes ingratiating; guilt elevates dissembling; eagerness for physical confrontation redeems parasitism.

Running: Health consciousness overpowers dissipation; stupidity undermines dissembling; indifference makes parasitism versatile.

Raincheck: Ulterior purposes ransom dissipation and dissembling; arbitrariness broadens the inventive potential for parasitism.

Depending on the customer's LOCATION, of course, there are innumerable possible variations on these conjunctions for the New York Giants Personality. In this example, as in any other that might spring to the human mind, the priority is that rationalization vindicate the anxious heart. Higher than that not even Dr. Alan Gibb and his Franchisement theory of playing the game of life can aim.

BIBLIOGRAPHY

What follows is a brief list of books dealing with Franchisement or authored by key figures in the Franchisement movement and its intellectual antecedents. If not available at your local bookstore, they may be purchased from counselors at the conclusion of a telephone consultation.

Adams, Abner. *All Those Darn Lies They Tell in Tennessee* (Capon Press, 1984).
———. *All Those Darn Lies They Tell in Kentucky* (Capon Press, 1989).
———. *All Those Darn Lies They Tell in West Virginia* (Capon Press, 1991).
———. *All That Goddamn Bullshit They Feed You in New York* (Abner Adams Publications, 1998).
Gibb, Alan. *You're a Peewee, I'm a Bambino* (Capon Press, 1992).
Herzl, Theodore. *The Dybbuk Called Peace* (New York Times Books, 1998).
La Rochefoucauld, Francois. *Memoirs* (Editions Temps Perdus, 1779).
Luderus, Walter. *Why the FBI Is My Life* (U.S. Government Printing House, 2002).
McElligott, Linda. *Omitive Language, Commitive Language—It's All Language* (Columbia University Press, 1993).
———. *Salsa—It's All Language* (Columbia University Press, 1999).
Rolf, Randy. *Randy Rolf: Unedited* (Capon Press, 1997).
———. *Randy Rolf: A Footnote* (Capon Press, 1999).
Schlesinger, Jr., Arthur. *The Age of Jackson* (Houghton Mifflin, 1955).
———. *From Jackson to Jack* (Houghton Mifflin, 1965).
———. *The Kennedys Before Franchisement* (Houghton Mifflin, 1998).
Sternheim, Joel. *Why There's So Much Open Beachfront and Nobody's Building on It Yet* (Information First Publishing, 1996).
Teller, Audrey. *What's So Colossal About the Colossus of Rhodes?* (Columbia University Press, 1968).
———. *The Pyramids: What They Say About the People Who Built Them, The People Who Visit Them, and the Animals That Live in Them* (Columbia University Press, 1970).

————. *The Pharos of Alexandria: Beacon of Light to the Ancient World* (Columbia University Press, 1972).

Willinger, Sidney. *1,000 New Solitaire Games* (University of Indians Press, 1990).

————. *When Winning Teams Are the Only Teams—Franchisement in Mass Culture* (University of Indiana Press, 1997).

Yevtushenko, Yevgeni. *Franchisement in the Post-Stalinist Era* (Kremlin Archives, published in 1997 but claimed by the author to have been written in 1966).

www.ingramcontent.com/pod-product-compliance
Lightning Source LLC
Chambersburg PA
CBHW020644250626
47154CB00008B/2805